HER
TRUSTED
HIGHLANDER

BOOK 1 OF THE MACKALLS OF DUNNET HEAD

JENNAE VALE

ISBN: 9780997006438

For my Family - David, Felicia and Jeff

Prologue

Malcolm Granger had come too far to let anyone stop him before he reached his goal. He could see an army of men off in the distance, being led by a woman with a streak of blue running through her otherwise white hair. They were charging towards him and all hell would be breaking loose shortly. His men already appeared panicked. He was the only one who could take control of the situation, which would allow him to retrieve the Twin Sword from its burial place in the rocky hillside and then use it to silence these highlanders forever. Once he had it in his hands they'd be hard pressed to stop him. The power of the sword was capable of bringing them all down, clearing the way for him to return home to San Francisco where he would use it to become the most powerful man on earth. Once back in his own time, not a soul would be able to stop him in his quest. They'd all be forced to bow down to him. Malcolm had built his empire with the incredible intelligence he possessed, but was never given the respect he felt he deserved. He'd been called every name in the book - nerd, geek, oddball. The world would pay for the disrespect they'd shown him from the time he was a child.

The explosives were set. All he needed now was to ignite the fuse and the rock wall before him would disintegrate into thousands of pieces. Malcolm had brought guns and explosives with him, knowing he might need them. And he had, having already shot someone who'd tried to get in his way. Surprisingly, he hadn't even hesitated and he'd do it again. He'd shoot as many of them as necessary if they tried to stop him. It didn't matter to him how many of them died, or if their deaths would affect the future. All that mattered was the sword. It would be his in a few short moments. Malcolm shouted orders to his men and then with one last glance over his shoulder to see where his opponents were, he set off the fuse. Rock shards and chunks rained down around him, as those nearby ran for cover. Malcolm didn't run. He stood his ground as every piece of flying rock missed him, landing at his feet and beside him.

Without waiting for things to settle down, Malcolm ran to the mouth of the cave. He could hear the loud rumble of horses arriving, carrying those who wished to put a halt to his victorious find, but he paid them no heed. No. Nothing could stop him now, nothing except witchcraft. One minute he was running towards the opening he'd created in the wall and the next everything went black.

1

Scotland 1514

Hands trembling, Kat wiped the bloody knife across the filthy white linens of her marriage bed. The adrenaline coursing through her veins spoke of the terror and revulsion gripping her with unexpected nausea. She stood staring at her husband as he lay wounded on the bed, blood staining the sheets and his nightshirt. As he cursed her and threatened her with bodily harm, images of his dirty fingernails clawing at her clothing, her hair, her breasts, caused her to retch what little food she had in her belly all over the floor. She had no way of knowing whether the injuries she'd caused him were life threatening and she didn't care. She'd wanted to kill him, but when she was done and he wasn't dead, she found she couldn't finish what she'd begun. All she could do now was run. Run for her life, because once he sounded the alarm they'd come after her and she knew she'd end up right back here beneath Bearach Calhoun.

Kat hurried from the wedding chamber, wearing only the now torn and tattered dress she'd been wearing earlier when, surrounded by strangers, she'd been forced to marry. If she hadn't been worried before, seeing their fearful and pitying glances as she was dragged in front of Laird Calhoun caused her to tremble in shocked dismay. How could this be happening to her? How could any of it be real? She forced her mind back to the present and down the passageway she shot and then to the stairs, through the doors and possibly to freedom. She needed a horse and the stables were just a short sprint across the courtyard, but what would she find when she got there. She could barely see her hand in front of her face it was so dark. The moon was completely hidden behind the clouds making it difficult for her to get her bearings, but giving her the cover she'd need in case anyone was out patrolling the courtyard. Grasping the knife in her hand, she ran blindly towards the entrance of the stables and then stopped. Kat flattened herself against the building and drew in a deep breath, slowly opening the doors only to find a young lad on the other side, staring wide-eyed at her as he took in her appearance and the sight of the knife in her hand. She had a moment of regret about what she must do. She didn't want to do it, but she had to. She put the knife to the lad's throat and attempted to be as menacing as possible.

"I need a horse. That one will do." She pointed to the large black steed in the first stall.

The boy eyed her warily, knees shaking. "That be Laird Calhoun's horse." He didn't move, instead staring at her, mouth agape.

Was he trying to be brave? God she hoped not, because if he was she'd be sunk. She couldn't possibly hurt him; she just hoped he didn't know that. Kat straightened her back and narrowed her eyes. "I don't care. Saddle him for me and be quick about it." She waved the knife in his direction, knowing that she was frightening him, but that was what she needed. She needed him to be so afraid that he'd do whatever she asked with no questions and no hesitation. Time was passing quickly and it would only be a short while before the whole castle would be awakened and then, if she wasn't already long gone, she'd be caught.

The lad did as she'd ordered and in moments the horse was ready and waiting for her. Keeping her eye on the lad, she quickly mounted and headed for the doors.

"Don't even think about sounding the alarm. You'll regret it if you do." Kat was doing her best to be as intimidating as possible, but she couldn't be sure it was working. Exiting the stables she scanned the courtyard. She could barely see, but it seemed no one was out and the gates were wide open and unguarded. The wedding feast had gone on long into the night and it was obvious that the guards were all so drunk that they'd just passed out where they stood. That might also explain why no one was looking for her yet.

Digging her heels into the horse and riding low over his neck, Kat bolted through the gates, down the road and through the village, sneaking quick peeks behind her as she went. She had no idea where she was or where she was going, but it didn't matter - getting away was her only goal. Somehow she'd find a way to get back home, but for now Kat needed to put as much time and space between herself and Laird Calhoun as she possibly could.

The moon peeked out from behind the clouds, lighting her way down the forested path she found herself on. Luck was on her side so far. No one appeared to be following her, but she couldn't stop, not even for a moment. Kat had been riding for hours and hadn't come across a single soul. That could work to her advantage, but at some point she really hoped she could find a place to get warm and spend the night. Still, it was probably just as well that she hadn't come across any cottages or even another village. She had no way of knowing how far ahead of her pursuers she might be. She hoped it would be many hours before anyone found the laird and the pursuit began in earnest. Not knowing was doing strange things to her. She found herself jumping at any noise near or far. Her horse had been strong and steady, controlling the great power she could feel beneath her. She was grateful he did because her riding skills were a bit rusty. She didn't even know his name, but she got the feeling he too was relieved to be away from Laird Calhoun. Kat rubbed his neck and bent forward to whisper her thanks into his ear.

The days were short now, making this night long and the air icy cold. Her fingers and feet were numb, making frostbite and hypothermia a very real possibility. She'd need to find a place to stop and warm herself, but being unfamiliar with her surroundings wasn't helping her. She might just freeze to death before she reached civilization. Kat had been in such a rush that she hadn't thought to take a cloak with her and now she was more than paying the price. Her teeth were chattering and it would be another hour or so before the sun rose in the sky and hopefully warmed her enough to prevent her becoming an ice statue. She would have cried, but any tears she shed would only freeze before they left her eyes.

Deciding to stop for a few moments, Kat dismounted and jumped up and down in an effort to warm herself. She noted the steam escaping her horse's nostrils and she placed her cold hands there, hoping it would thaw her fingers. The steed flinched at her icy touch, but Kat soothed him with some quiet cooing. He nuzzled her with his nose and Kat wrapped her arms around his big neck, hoping some of his body heat would transfer to her.

Hopelessness was beginning to seep in along with the cold. She wanted to scream so badly at the predicament she found herself in, but she refrained, thinking her pursuers might hear, and it would lead them directly to her.

What a mess she had gotten herself into. Kat didn't even know how it had all happened. Yes, she did. She knew exactly how it had happened. It was *why* that boggled her mind. Why was she here? Why was this happening to her?

Shouts in the distance had her jumping back on her horse and urging him forward into a gallop. She'd given herself a headache just thinking about everything that had happened and this frantic pace they were now traveling at wasn't helping any. Kat gazed up through the treetops as a new wave of despair overtook her. And then, as if things weren't bad enough, the first flakes of a winter storm silently drifted to the ground.

2

It had been snowing all day and damned if he hadn't forgotten what that could be like. Beautiful, to be sure, but it also meant the temperature had to be frigid enough for those gentle flakes of white to fall. He pulled his hooded cape tightly around his head, feeling the icy breeze more acutely than he might have in the past. He'd better get used to this weather quickly because it would be months before it was warm again.

Nick had spent the last few years of his life in a land and time far, far away from his beloved Scotland. San Francisco wasn't known for its frigid climate or snowfall and that was one thing he'd rather enjoyed about his stay five hundred years in the future.

Excitement spurred him on as he headed home to his beloved family. They surely must think him long dead. He chuckled to himself as he thought of the reception he'd receive upon his arrival. His brothers and hunting companions, Rory and Duncan, after their initial shock would likely crush him in bear hugs along with his two youngest brothers, Aidan and Lockie. His mother surely would shed a tear or two, as would his sisters. He was sorry for the suffering she must have endured thinking her oldest bairn lost to her forever. The happy images of his homecoming continued to play out in his mind, after all, what else did he have to do but daydream on this long ride home.

More images formed in his mind - a beautiful young woman, his betrothed, Skye Maguire. Had she waited for him? He wondered why she would. Theirs was not a love match, at least not for him, but if she had waited, he would do his duty and marry her for the good of his clan.

The dappled light shining through the trees was angled such that he knew it would soon disappear and he'd be forced to spend yet another night camping here in these woods. The days were shorter at this time of year and the sun set earlier and earlier every day.

Sizing up the situation, Nick decided he'd ride a bit further before finding a spot to set up camp. He had enough food to last him until he reached home, and the thought of all the work involved in creating a shelter and a fire to keep warm, had him rethinking his decision to ride on. If he stopped now, he'd still reach home by nightfall tomorrow. He drew his horse to a stop and surveyed his surroundings. Noting some fallen tree branches he could use to create a shelter on a relatively dry patch of ground convinced Nick this would be a good place to spend the night.

As he prepared to dismount, Laoch spooked, jumping and planting all four hooves firmly on the ground, ready to run. Nick whispered soft, calming words and stroked his steed's tense neck. Pricked straight forward, his horse's ears were an indicator of the direction the perceived threat was coming from. Sitting as quietly as possible, Nick searched for the source of his horse's anxiety, his eyes taking in every inch of the wooded area around him. He listened closely for anything out of the ordinary and then he heard it, the sounds of a horse galloping his way and shortly he saw both horse and rider barreling in his direction. The rider continuously looked behind as if being chased. Nick was prepared to take action should he need to, but patience was best in these situations. Why react before he knew exactly what he was reacting to. As the rider approached, Nick realized it was a woman. She had a determined expression on her face as she crouched low over her horse's neck, charging directly at him. Nick placed his horse squarely in her way in an effort to stop her. If she needed help, he was sure he could assist her, no matter what she was fleeing from. Her golden hair caught the last glimmers of light as they filtered through the trees and he saw that she wore no cloak for warmth. She would freeze to death when she stopped to rest. There were no villages or crofts anywhere in this area where she could seek refuge. He knew because he had just ridden an entire day without seeing another soul.

As the woman galloped closer, Nick waved his arms in the air to catch her attention. She didn't notice as she was focused on whoever was chasing her. Her horse, however, came to a screeching halt, tossing his head in the air and then rearing. The rider, unprepared, tumbled to the ground cursing much like the women Nick had known in San Francisco.

"What do you think you're doing?" she fumed as she rose from the ground and dusted herself off. Kat grabbed her horse's reins and prepared to mount the skittish equine. "Whoa! Whoa!"

"Is everything alright?" the very tall and handsome man atop the chestnut steed asked. "Who are you fleeing from?"

How on earth did he know she was running away? "I don't think that's any of your damn business," Kat didn't have time for introductions or conversation, she had to get moving and quickly. She'd ridden through what had remained of the night before and now this entire day. She wasn't sure how much progress she'd made, but she certainly didn't have the luxury of standing here chatting with this stranger. Her *husband* and his men would be after her. Unfortunately, in her haste to get away, she hadn't done enough damage to the vile man to keep him from pursuing her.

"My name is Nick Mackall," the man introduced himself.

Kat didn't answer him, instead continuing her efforts to calm her horse, who maddeningly refused to stand still. He pulled backwards to get away and Kat found herself being dragged down the path in the direction she'd just come. "Whoa! Stop!" she yelled to no avail as the horse reared, crow-hopped and tried to spin away from her. She planted her feet, but her small frame was no match for the giant steed who was continuing to drag her. Her foot caught on a root and she fell face first in a pile of snow, letting the horse go before she got dragged across the ground behind him. "Damn it!" She turned, ready to run on foot and instead ran directly into a very solid man, who steadied her with his hands on her arms and a smile on his lips.

"Do you mind telling me who you're running from?" he asked.

Kat bristled in his arms, looking up at him through stormy eyes. "Let me go. I have to run. He'll kill me if he finds me, or worse." She tried to break free, but his firm grasp held her in place.

"What could be worse, lass?" He gazed down at her with an amused expression.

"Do you really need to ask? Just let me go, please." Again she tried to wrench herself free.

"I can't in good conscience allow ye to run off into the woods without a cloak or a horse, now can I?" He tipped his head and cocked an eyebrow in her direction.

"Yeah. Well thanks for your concern, but it's your fault that I find myself without a horse." She stared angrily into his eyes, triumphant in the knowledge that she'd stated the obvious.

"Point taken, and I apologize, lass. Perhaps I can be of service. As I said before, my name is Nick Mackall, and ye'd be…"

"Kat," she said, indignantly wiping the snow from her clothes. "Katriona."

"Well, Katriona, I'm about to set up camp for the night. A warm fire would do ye some good." His warm smile was somewhat disarming, but she wasn't about to let herself be fooled by this charming stranger.

She was shivering violently now and Nick removed his cape and wrapped her in it. The warmth it carried from his body felt good to her and her legs almost gave way beneath her. "Thank you," she uttered through chattering teeth.

"Come here, lass." He pulled her into his arms and began vigorously stroking her back in what she assumed was an effort to warm her.

"I'm fine. There's really no need for that." She wrestled herself from his grasp and immediately regretted it as she felt the cold air sweep up inside the cloak. She was about to speak again, when the sound of horses galloping towards them became apparent. "I have to hide. Please don't tell them you know where I am." Panic filled her eyes as she spun in circles searching for a place to conceal herself.

"I wouldnae think of it, lass." His eyes scanned the area. "Come with me." He took her by the arm and led her away from the road. She followed along beside him and he pulled apart the branches of a very large evergreen bush. "Ye'll need to give me my cloak for a moment. We don't want them questioning why I'm out here in the middle of nowhere unprotected from the cold, now do we?"

Kat reluctantly removed the cloak and squeezed into the space inside the bush, which Nick then covered with more brush. "We'll hope they dinnae stop for long." And then he walked away from her. Peeking out from her shelter, she watched as he made his way back to his horse, brushing away the tracks they'd just made in the snow.

Trust was not something she had a lot of lately, but Kat didn't feel she had any choice other than to put her faith in this stranger. She hoped he wouldn't betray her once he knew what she was running from. The sounds of horses and men drew closer and finally came to a stop.

Kat held her breath and listened for any sign they'd discovered her.

Nick lifted his horse's hoof in an effort to appear as if he were cleaning them. He held his ground and waited for the approaching men to come to a halt. From the looks of them they were quite determined to hunt their quarry until they found her.

"Good day to ye." Nick placed Laoch's hoof back on the ground and directed his greeting to the apparent leader of the group. "Where are ye off to in such a hurry?"

"We're searching for our laird's wife." The disheveled appearance of the man's clothing spoke of their haste in pursuing Katriona.

"Did she run away?" Nick did his best to appear aghast at the thought.

"Why would ye think that?" the man asked, suddenly suspicious.

"It's fairly obvious. Six men riding quickly through the forest are-nae searching for someone who's lost now are they?" Nick adjusted his saddle as he awaited a response.

The man gave this some thought and then, letting down his guard, nodded. "Aye, she's run. She stabbed him in his sleep and was long gone before we found him."

"I'm sorry to hear it. Does he still live?" Nick asked, doing his best to sound concerned.

"Aye. His injury is nae so great and he's a strong one. He'll survive, I've nae doubt." The man sat up straighter in his saddle, eyes searching the roadside.

"'Tis good to hear. I know 'tis none of my business, but why would the lass run?" Nick grabbed the man's attention before he had a chance to examine Kat's hiding place too carefully.

"She was scairt of her wedding night." The men all laughed and exchanged crude comments.

"Stabbing yer husband seems a rather extreme measure to avoid yer wedding night. Are ye sure there wasnae another reason?" Nick raised an eyebrow in disbelief.

"Nae. The laird told us all of what happened. She's a feisty wench and rather than submit to her husband, she tried to kill him."

"Where do ye think the lass ran off to?" Any information Nick could gather would be useful in helping Katriona.

"We're nae sure. We've been following her tracks."

She looks to be heading towards MacKenzie lands, but she would be on foot now. We caught her rider-less horse as it ran back towards home." He nodded his head in the direction of Katriona's horse as he spoke.

Nick was thankful that the now heavily falling snow had done an excellent job of covering Kat's tracks. The men on horseback had done their part as well. They had all congregated in the exact spot where her horse had skittered about and then run. They'd have no way of knowing she huddled safely nearby. "If she's on foot, ye'll nae doubt find her quickly I would think."

"The snow has made tracking difficult. We're nae sure if she lies somewhere injured or if she escaped unscathed. Did ye see anything out of the ordinary in yer travels?"

"I did see a lass on horseback. It was on this path." Nick pointed back the way he'd just come. "She passed me at a walk perhaps about an hour ago. I stopped to talk, but she didnae do more than nod in greeting and continue on her way. I thought it strange at the time - a woman alone, riding through these woods, especially with a storm brewing, but she appeared to know where she was going, so I continued on my way and didnae give it another thought."

"Why did ye nae say something before this?" The man appeared suspicious again.

"I wanted to be sure ye werenae after her for the wrong reasons, but I can see now that we've spoken that the lass deserves to be caught and brought back to her husband. What do ye think he'll do when he has her back?"

"Beat her for certain and then bed the wench. After that he'll surely punish her for daring to take a blade to him. Time in the dungeon should teach her to mind her ways."

"Well, ye'd best be off then if yer to find her before dark. I'd offer to help, but my horse is spent after our long day of travel. Ye wouldn't be interested in selling the lass's horse to me, would ye? I'd like to continue on, but I'd like to give this one some rest." Nick nodded towards his horse.

"I'm afraid not, this be the laird's prize stud she stole. He'll be wanting him back, mayhap more than the lass. As fer yer kind offer of help, we'll not be in need." He turned and spoke to his men. "Daylight is waning, lads. We'd best be off. If this lass causes us any more trouble than she already has, she'll have more to fear than the laird."

The men kicked their horses into a gallop and sped past Nick, who avoiding the spray of snow from the horses, prayed they'd disappear from sight quickly so he could get Katriona safely wrapped in his cloak once again.

Kat's teeth were chattering so loudly, she feared the men would hear. *Why does he continue to engage them in conversation?* She feared this Nick Mackall would turn her over to her pursuers once he knew what had really happened, but although he'd sympathized with their plight, he hadn't betrayed her. He'd even tried to get her horse back, to no avail. The sounds of horses galloping off and then plodding footsteps nearing her hiding spot told her she was safe once again. Or at least she hoped she was. She knew nothing about this Nick person, or what his ulterior motive might be for aiding her. Would he expect payment? She had nothing to offer. The bushes rattled noisily as they were being pushed aside.

"You can come out now. They're gone." Nick offered her his hand, but she ignored it and pushed and shoved her way out of the tight spot she had been hunkered down in. Before she could speak, the cape was thrown around her shoulders once again and Nick was rubbing warmth into her back and arms. She didn't struggle to get away this time. "We'll need to move on from here. Somewhere off the road would be best. I've nae doubt they'll be back when they cannae find ye."

Her jaw seemed to be wired shut, but in fact it was the cold that had rendered her muscles tight and immovable. It took every ounce of strength she had to open it to speak. "I'll be fine on my own. You needn't worry about me."

Nick laughed out loud. "Don't be stubborn or daft, lass. Ye willnae get far. Those men are determined to find ye and I don't care to think what they'll do to ye when that happens. Now, come with me." He draped an arm casually around her shoulder. "Ye've nothing to fear from me." Lifting her chin, he looked deeply into her eyes and she noted the tawny gold color of his, flecked as they were with copper, green and brown. "Perhaps I'm the one who should be scairt." He laughed once again, irritating her with his good humor, but she followed along at his side anyway. What choice did she have? That was a question she'd been asking herself a lot lately.

3

Having Katriona seated snugly on his lap had its advantages and disadvantages. The advantage being it was keeping them both warm. The disadvantage being it was warming parts of Nick that he would prefer remain unawakened. He shifted in the saddle trying to move back away from contact with her, but as soon as he did, she snuggled right back into him. Katriona was sleeping soundly in his arms and was unaware of the torment she was causing him and glad of that he was. The poor lass had been through quite enough for one day and the last thing he wanted was for her to fear his intentions towards her.

He remembered hearing about Bearach Calhoun in the days prior to his disappearance and none of what he'd heard had been good. The man had a reputation for brutalizing those who served him and those unfortunate enough to find themselves in his employ feared him greatly. He'd allowed his castle and property to fall into disrepair and it was widely known that he sought a wife to bear him sons and to get his castle in order.

Not a soul dared offer their daughter to the man, fearing what might happen to her in his household. This had angered Calhoun, who had become a nuisance to his neighbors by raiding their lands and kidnapping young women from the crofters cottages and forcing himself on them and then when he tired of them, sending them home to their families broken and battered. As he gazed down at Katriona, his heart ached at the thought of Calhoun harming her and hoped that the effects of such abuse would not be long lasting.

The final vestiges of light were fading and the snow had ceased falling, so now would be the perfect time to stop and make camp for the night. Dismounting would be tricky. Nick didn't wish to awaken Katriona, but he simply had to. There was no way to gracefully dismount and hold her all at the same time. "Katriona." He bent his head to softly speak her name into her ear. "Katriona." He added a little shake. She was apparently a sound sleeper. Her steady, even breathing told him she was not about to wake. Somehow he managed to get his leg over the horse and jump to the ground, all the while holding his charge. He smiled at his own abilities and gave himself a mental pat on the back.

Spying a large evergreen tree, Nick cradled Katriona within the trunk and large protruding roots, which made a perfect little nook for her. He covered her with his cape and set about gathering wood for a fire. Once he had completed that task and the flames were blazing, he found a low branch conveniently placed above Katriona's head. Nick retrieved a plaid from his saddlebag and draped it over the protruding limb, creating a tent. A few well-placed stones held it in place, close enough to the fire to enjoy it's warmth, but far enough away to avoid the plaid catching fire. Retrieving a griddle, a bag of oats, some dried fruit and a flask of cider, Nick quickly put together a meal. Bannocks never tasted so good to him. He ate all that he made and then made more for Katriona, who still slept peacefully. Observing her now, he noted the way her long dark lashes brushed the very top of her cheeks, which held a rosy glow from the warmth of the fire. He had the urge to touch her face as she slept. He longed to feel the softness he new he'd find there, but instead he called her name. "Katriona." His voice came out louder and gruffer than he'd intended.

She grimaced and attempted to change positions, but she nearly fell over in the process and startled herself awake. "Where am I?" her worried voice shook with fear.

"Here. Safe with me." Nick reached out a hand to gently lay it on her foot, which peeked out from beneath the cape he'd swaddled her in and then he carefully pulled the cape over her foot. She quickly pulled it from his grasp. "I've made some food fer ye. Surely ye must be quite hungry by now."

She glanced around the campsite and her gaze fell on Nick, who suddenly felt quite at odds with himself.

Katriona was a married woman and he had no right to see her through lust-filled eyes. Add to that the fact that he was possibly to be married himself when he returned home and he counted himself a total arse for the thoughts that had been spinning through his head. "Why have we stopped? They're bound to find me."

The panic in her voice left him no choice but to attempt to comfort her. He took some bannocks and the cider and joined her in the makeshift tent. "I won't let any harm come to ye. Ye have my word." He helped her to sit up and get more comfortable and once the look of worry on her pretty face had dissipated, he handed her the bannocks. "Here, eat. Ye'll need yer strength. We'll have a long ride ahead of us on the morrow."

"Tomorrow? Where are we going?" She took a tentative bite out of the bannock and apparently found it tolerably edible, because she took another bite and then another. He held out the flask and she greedily drank the cider, dripping some down her chin in the process.

Nick wiped the cider away with his thumb and noted that she flinched when his hand came near. On closer examination, he could see bruises on her neck and face, which he hadn't noticed before. He'd had her bundled in his cape almost from the moment they'd met. She'd had her back to him as they rode, so he had not had the opportunity to take a close look. "I won't hurt ye. I've already promised ye I wouldn't. I'm a man of my word.

Ye've no need to fear me. I can see though why ye may fear yer husband.

Katriona pulled the cape up around her throat to cover the marks she bore. "How do I know I can trust you? I made the mistake not too long ago of trusting a man who said he'd help me, but he lied. How do I know you're not lying?" The fierce expression on her face forced Nick to hold back the smile he felt coming on at her obvious attempt at standing up to him.

"I guess ye dinnae." Nick pondered this problem for a moment or two before speaking again. "I understand that yer trust has been shaken by yer experiences, but I can do nothing to prove myself to ye right now. I can only promise ye that I will not lay a mean hand upon ye and I'll see ye safely to my family home in Dunnet Head. Once yer there, ye'll have my family to care fer ye. Ye dinnae ken this, but as I've already told ye, I'm a man of my word. Ye'll ken it soon enough."

Kat stared at him through narrow, suspicious eyes. She wanted to trust him, but she didn't know if she'd ever be able to trust anyone again after what she'd just been through. He had a gentle look to him and a ready smile. He was a charmer and quite handsome as well. At about six foot four, with tousled brown locks and those unbelievable tawny eyes, he was definitely her type, but not here. Not now. She still couldn't understand how she found herself in this place and time. How was it possible that she was examining medieval artifacts in the Scottish highlands as part of her work for billionaire Malcolm Granger, when she suddenly and very inexplicably fell through time to find herself in sixteenth-century Scotland, alone and unprepared for what was to come next?

Glancing around the camp, she noted where everything was located, including Nick's horse. If it was at all possible, she would escape tonight. Her only thought was to get to civilization. Perhaps if she got to Edinburgh, she could figure out a way to get back home to her own century and at the very least she thought she'd be safe from Bearach Calhoun. Kat didn't have time to waste traveling through the highlands with this man and then living with his family. How could that be any better than the situation she'd just left? She was a prisoner, no matter how she looked at it, unless she could take matters into her own hands. It wouldn't be easy, but she'd wait for her chance and then seize it. She'd, of course, be leaving Nick alone in the woods without transportation, but that couldn't be helped.

"Yer giving me the evil eye, lass. What is it that yer thinking?" He smiled warmly at her, but she was unable to return his smile.

"I'm debating about whether or not I should trust you." She tipped her head to examine him more closely.

"And yer conclusion?" Nick tipped his own head to match her and eyed her with a teasing glint in his eye.

"You're quite charming, Mr. Mackall, but I've learned a valuable lesson these past several days." She fussed with the cape and averted her gaze.

"And that is?" Nick was obviously aware of her discomfort and was doing his best to win her over.

"And that is, not to trust someone until they give you a reason to trust them. You haven't given me a good enough reason yet."

"Time will give ye yer proof, Katriona. I dinnae doubt ye'll trust me before verra long." He smiled confidently at her.

"The jury's still out on that one, mister." She continued eating the food he'd given her. It was either very good, or she was very hungry. Probably the latter she thought. She practically bit her tongue when she realized she may have just used language that would call attention to her true origins. He was gazing at her with a curious expression, or perhaps she was just being paranoid.

Nick made himself comfortable next to her in the tiny shelter, re-adjusting the cape and covering them both.

"Just what do you think you're doing?" He wasn't thinking of sleeping with her, was he?

"This may nae be to yer liking, lass, but I'm going to sleep in here with ye tonight. We'll need each other's body heat so we dinnae freeze." He continued making himself comfortable next to her.

"And what would you be doing if I wasn't with you?" *Now I see what he's up to. He's got me here alone in the middle of nowhere and he thinks he can just have his way with me. Well he's got another thing coming.*

"I'd have my cape and that blanket to keep me warm." He gestured with his hands towards both items.

He had her there. She could force him to sleep by the fire, but that hardly seemed right. "Fine, but keep your hands and other body parts to yourself."

"As ye wish, m'lady." He leaned back against the tree, arms folded across his chest and closed his eyes.

Kat waited for him to fall asleep and then planned on giving it a bit more time before she put her plan in motion.

The lass was up to something. He was sure of it. He was a light sleeper, so whatever she was about, he'd know it quickly enough to stop it. He'd slept fitfully and uncomfortably for a few hours when he felt her move away from him. At first little by little she put space between them. He kept his eyes closed, curious to see what she was going to do. Next he felt the cape slowly moving across his body. Once it was completely removed, he moved onto his side, facing her, eyes stilled closed. Katriona became very still and waited. Exactly what he would've done if he were her. She made her move shortly thereafter and crept out of the tent. He peeked through one open eye to see her heading for his horse. She glanced around trying to find a way to mount the eighteen-hand beast and spying a nearby tree stump, silently led the horse to it and with some difficulty mounted the horse bareback.

This was a disaster waiting to happen. "Where do ye think yer going to, lass?"

Katriona jumped at the sound of his voice and quickly glanced over her shoulder at Nick, urging the horse forward into a gallop. "I'm sorry," she yelled as she sped out of their camp.

Nick almost laughed. He'd gotten Laoch from the MacKenzies who'd trained all their horses to return to them with just a whistle. He had to get her back before she hurt herself and the horse. Galloping through a heavily wooded area was never a good idea. Placing his fingers in his mouth he let loose a loud shrill whistle and watched as the horse spun back his way. Katriona had all she could do to hold on, but she did and he could hear her cursing all the way back.

"Damn you," she yelled as the horse came to a dead stop right in front of Nick.

"Damn me? Ye were the one stealing my horse." Nick reached up and pulled her kicking and screaming from the horse's back. Once her feet hit the ground he let her go. "I've told ye I'll not harm ye and I meant it. I ken ye dinnae believe me, but that is nae fer me to worry over." Nick took the horse from her and began saddling him. "Now that ye've had me wake the dead with my whistle, we'd best be moving on. If those that chase ye are nearby, they likely heard me and will begin their search early."

Nick quickly gathered all of his things and put them in the saddlebag. Once everything was ready, he mounted his horse and held a hand out to Katriona, which she reluctantly took. He pulled her up to sit behind him. "Ye'd best hold on to me. We'll be riding at a good clip until I'm sure we're safe. Without the falling snow, we'll have nothing to cover our tracks."

Katriona gingerly placed her hands around Nick's waist, but once he urged his horse forward, she tightened her hold to keep from falling. He smiled to himself. This lass would not get the better of him, no matter how hard she might try.

4

Teeth chattering and hands like blocks of ice, Katriona managed to squeeze out from between locked jaws, "Can we stop, please?"

They had just arrived at a small icy creek. It wasn't completely frozen over, but the areas near the banks showed signs of ice here and there.

"We'll cross first and then we'll stop for a short while. Laoch needs water and a rest, as do we." Nick expertly guided the horse to a low spot in the creek and urged the skeptical horse across. Once on the other side, he dismounted after prying Katriona's hands loose from his waist. He reached up to help her down, but her feet were so cold, she could barely feel them beneath her and she wobbled on them as they touched the ground. Nick steadied her and guided her to a nearby rock. "Sit here. I'll get a small fire going to warm ye and while I do, mayhap ye can tell me why yer running away."

Katriona had expertly avoided this subject until now, by sleeping or being in a genuinely bad mood, but she imagined she should give him some sort of explanation. The truth was pretty unbelievable, but she could doctor it up so that she only told him the things that would make sense. "There's not much to tell," she started.

"Where are ye from?" Nick asked. He had gathered some wood and dried brush and placed it in a clear spot near where she sat. As he knelt and got to work, he occasionally glanced up at her, awaiting his answer.

"Edinburgh." That was partly true. She had been born there, but grew up in London and until only recently, still lived there. If anything, she hoped to get to Edinburgh in order to seek help to get back to her own time. Where she might find that help was another question she hadn't yet answered.

"Ye dinnae sound like yer from Edinburgh," Nick noted.

"Well, that's because I was born there, but raised in London." *That should satisfy his curiosity.*

"And how did ye get all this way from London?" He was trying to lead her into telling him her story and she was busy rewriting it in her head.

"I was traveling with my family and we were on our way to visit relatives in Sutherland when we were attacked by highwaymen." Was that the correct term for them? Would they have been called that in the sixteenth century? She wished she could be sure. The last thing she wanted was to draw his suspicion. Kat was an expert in medieval artifacts. She could identify every pot, sword, shoe or shield, why it was used and who would have used it, but since being transported to this time period she'd had more than one moment of doubt about her knowledge of the time. She was second guessing everything she said and did, fearing the outcome for her if she were wrong.

"I see." Nick had an ember started and was blowing on it to get the fire going. After a moment or two, it flared up and the surrounding brush and wood were engulfed in flames.

Katriona breathed a sigh of relief as she moved closer to the fire, practically putting her frozen feet on the flames. To her surprise and before she could stop him, Nick grabbed her feet and removing her boots, placed them near the fire. He began vigorously rubbing her feet to get her blood circulating. "Thank you." That *was* really nice of him and while it was an odd thing for a stranger to do for her, she was grateful.

"Back to yer story, lass. I'm fascinated to this point." Was he being serious or was he teasing her? He continued warming her feet and when he was done, put her lovely warmed boots back on and reached for her hands, which she gladly let him take. His hands were large and warm and the heat he was creating with the friction of rubbing them was astonishing, but very much appreciated.

"Well, I ran and hid in the brush," she continued. "Everyone was killed, but the highwaymen couldn't find me. I could hear them yelling to each other as they searched and then they fled for fear of being discovered, taking all of our belongings with them. I didn't know what to do or where to go. I was terrified, so I continued wandering through the woods. Night fell and I curled myself into a ball to sleep. At some point during the night I felt a boot nudging my thigh. I opened my eyes to see a man standing over me." From this point on, the story she would share was true. "I was terrified, thinking the men had come back to kill me too, but this man, Earnan Gibb was his name, reassured me that he wouldn't hurt me, much as you did and I, being desperate for help, believed him. He told me he'd help me get to safety and I again believed him." Her voice took on an angry edge. "Little did I know that he planned to sell me to Bearach Calhoun for a small fortune. The Laird apparently needed a wife and for reasons which quickly became apparent, I now understand why no one would have him." She gazed up into Nick's very interested face and was drawn in by the warmth of his gaze, losing her train of thought.

"Go on," Nick encouraged.

"Where was I?" She was in serious trouble here. Nick Mackall and his feet and hand rubbing, along with that face and that physique, were having a very curious effect on her.

"Bearach Calhoun needed a wife," Nick reminded her. "Oh, right. Well, you see, he needs an heir and so, since no one else would have him, he bought me from Earnan Gibb and I was forced to marry him. On our wedding night, I had about all that I could stand, so I refused him, what according to him were his husbandly rights. Besides being a vile and disgusting human being, he is also a very violent man and he beat me when I told him it would be a cold day in hell before I allowed him to touch me. I have the marks all over my body to prove it, as you've seen."

"And ye tried to kill the man." It wasn't so much a question as a statement.

"I tried, but unfortunately, I failed. I was scared to death and I decided to run while I could still get away. I stole a horse and I don't even know which direction I headed in. All I knew was that I had to get away. If he catches me, I'm afraid of what he'll do to me." She stared into the flames, no longer even aware of the warmth slowly thawing her extremities.

"That is quite the tale," Nick wrapped her in the plaid from his saddle bag. "I'm going to boil some water. I've some food in my bags. I'll get it for ye."

Kat sat perfectly still, reliving the nightmare of Laird Calhoun and her wedding night. Hopelessness was a feeling she'd had a lot over the last few days, but Nick was giving her back a glimmer of hope as he took care of her now. Her jaded heart found it hard to believe he was really going to help her and that he wasn't perhaps exactly the same as the man who had offered her aid that night in the woods. What could she do? He wouldn't let her get away and he was taking her some-where - to his home, he said. Only time would tell what awaited her; she hoped it would be as Nick had promised her.

"We'll be at my home before dark and then ye'll have a full belly and a warm bed. Ye need to rest and me mother and sisters will be happy to see to yer care." Nick was concerned as he watched Katriona sit silently, staring into the flames. She had been through a horrible ordeal and mentally she appeared to be struggling to deal with it. It was obvious she didn't fully trust him and now that he'd heard her story, he understood why. He'd do his best to be gentle and kind, causing her not a moment's worry, if he could. "Was it all of yer family that ye lost that day, lass?"

"Yes. All of them." Her answer was short and clipped.

Poor lass must still be in shock. Nick couldn't imagine how painful that must be for her. He hadn't seen his family in over two years, but they were still alive and well, or at least he hoped so. The excitement he felt at seeing them again was tempered by the fact that Katriona would never have the experience of seeing her family ever again. He'd be careful not to upset her with talk of the Mackalls. "I'm so verra sorry, lass." And he was.

Katriona acknowledged him with a slight nod of her head, which she then dropped to her chest in obvious sorrow.

Leaving her side, Nick retrieved a small pot and filled it with water from the creek. He placed it in the flames and then sat back down beside Katriona. He wanted to place a reassuring arm around her shoulder, but he doubted she'd allow it, so instead he sat as close as he could without making her feel uncomfortable.

Katriona surprisingly slumped into his side and he found that he had no choice but to put his arm around her to comfort her. She sniffled quietly into his shoulder and he stroked her hair with his free hand. "'Tis all right, lass. I'm here. I willnae allow anyone to harm ye."

Kat wasn't sure what to do with her hands, so she folded them in her lap. She was feeling quite safe and secure in the arms of this strong highlander. When he told her he wouldn't allow anyone to hurt her, she believed him wholeheartedly. Maybe she *could* trust this man. She'd reserve judgment for just a while longer. If he was true to his word and he brought her to his home without incident, then she'd rethink this whole trust issue she had.

She gazed up at him through tear-filled eyes and was surprised to meet his concerned face, staring down at her. He tipped her chin up with his finger. His eyes were saying something she couldn't quite read, but they were saying it with an intensity she hadn't seen before now and she quickly glanced down. She didn't have a lot of experience with men, so reading them was beyond her capability. Her job kept her pretty busy and so her social life was lacking. The only men she knew were the ones she worked with and none of them were at all appealing to her. Joel Prewitt, her immediate supervisor asked her out a few times and she'd gone. As her best friend Allie always told her, you'll never know if you don't put yourself out there. Joel was sweet, but he was also not the strong man she wanted and needed. He was terrified of their boss, Malcolm Granger, and would never stand up for himself. Katriona felt badly for him. He worked his butt off for the man, but never got any recognition for it and instead usually was left feeling as if he were going to be fired at any moment. Mr.

Granger had always been pleasant to her, but he was also condescending in his treatment because she was a woman and in *his* corporate world, she couldn't possibly measure up to the men who worked for him. Not that she wanted to move up in the company. She enjoyed being out in the field. That was her passion, not sitting in an office and being yelled at by her boss.

Nick disentangled himself from her and checked on the water. "I think that's hot enough," he offered, wrapping his cape around the handle and removing it from the fire. He briefly placed it in the icy creek. Kat was fascinated. He'd just taken all that time to heat the water, why was he putting it in the creek. She realized as he handed it to her, it had been to cool the pan and the water just enough for her to drink. The warm water felt wonderful as it hit her mouth and then her throat. She was so cold, she couldn't imagine ever being warm again.

"Is that better?" Nick asked, a worried expression crossing his face.

"Yes, much." She handed the small pot back to him and he drank from it and then gave it back to her. "Thank you for all of this." Her gratitude was heartfelt and she wanted to make it clear to him.

"There's no need to thank me. What kind of man would I be if I had left ye alone to fend fer yerself in the woods?" He smiled, lighting up his face and she thought how handsome he was. She didn't want to be attracted to him. Hadn't he told her he was to marry? Besides, she was probably just feeling grateful to him for saving her. It would pass as soon as she found herself among other people. And what then? That was the question; just how was she going to find her way back to her own time, or was she doomed to stay here forever? The thought made her shudder and Nick, mistaking it for her being cold, pulled her close and covered as much of her as he could with his cape and body.

Nick was feeling inexplicably attracted to this young woman. She was a beauty. He'd recognized that when he'd first set eyes on her, but there was something else about her that attracted him. She was obviously a damsel in distress, but that couldn't be it, because despite the fact that she needed his help, she was a strong woman who obviously had taken her escape from servitude into her own hands. She needed him right now, but he knew that as soon as they found their way safely to Dunaill, she would have plenty of others to be of assistance and he would cease to be the rock to which she attached herself.

He couldn't deny he was enjoying the way she leaned into him as they sat by the fire. Touching her feet and hands had brought him sensations that travelled from his hands to his heart and then throughout the rest of his body, which then found him sitting awkwardly in order to conceal his body's reaction to the closeness he was feeling with Kat. He found that despite the fact they'd just met and he really knew very little about her, he liked her and he wanted to know everything about her.

He'd need patience though. She did not seem the type of lass who would tell him all her secrets so soon. The women he'd met in San Francisco had been the exact opposite, telling him every little detail of their lives and leaving Nick wishing he was anywhere but with them.

What was he thinking, he was to be married. Or at least he thought he was. Two years was a long time for someone to wait for a person who had disappeared. For all he knew, they'd given up on him. Thought him dead. He'd know soon enough. Nick imagined as soon as he got home, word would spread to the surrounding areas that he had returned and his wife-to-be would hear that he was back and if she hadn't found another, his fate would be sealed. The thought of it made him sad and he was sadder still when he looked down and found Kat gazing up at him with the sweetest expression. He wondered what she was thinking, but didn't dare to ask.

"We should go." Nick gathered their things and then led Katriona to the horse. He mounted and this time he pulled her up in front of him. "'Twill be much easier for me to keep ye warm this way," he said, by way of explanation. Katriona didn't seem to mind one bit as she settled in and rested her head on his chest. Nick couldn't lie. He was enjoying the feel of her body so close to his. This was going to be one enjoyably torturous ride to his family castle in Dunnet Head.

5

Malcolm Granger awoke in a most confused state. He had no idea where he was or, for that matter, how he'd gotten there. His arms and legs felt as stiff as stone, and as he tentatively moved them, he heard the sounds of crumbling rock hitting the ground. A light shone from behind him and with great effort he turned his head to see a sword glowing with an iridescence which lit the cavern and cast out the darkness from every corner. *The sword... The Twin Sword!* He'd been searching for it for most of his adult life and here it was, entombed in this rock prison along with him. Piecing together the fragments of memory he could recall, Malcolm remembered he'd time-travelled from twenty-first century San Francisco to sixteenth-century Scotland with the express purpose of finding this sword. He'd snuck through the portal of fog created when that Scottish bastard, Nick Mackall, travelled back to his own time. His memory was cloudy as to the details - how did he come to be locked in this dark cave with the glowing sword he'd come to retrieve? His memory was not serving him well at this point, but the one thing he did know was he wanted that sword and it was now within easy reach. Now that he'd found it, how would he ever be able to get out of this tomb? He had to get out and return to the twenty-first century with his prize. That would mean breaking through these stone walls and then finding Mackall and forcing him to bring him back to San Francisco.

He rubbed his arms and found that more bits of stone hit the ground. His memory returned with a force so great, he thought his head might explode. The witch!

She's the one who locked him in here. Yes. She'd turned him into a stone statue and enclosed him in this cave with the Twin Sword. It was all coming back to him now. If he ever got out of here, she'd surely pay. He'd see to it, because he'd have the sword and it would give him all the power he'd ever dreamed possible. He took a few tentative steps towards the sword. Would he be able to touch it? He extended his shaking hands towards it and he felt the air thicken the closer he came to it. He reached for it again, but no matter how close he got, he always seemed to hit an invisible wall. Malcolm sat down on the ground in front of it, contemplating what to do next. He was freezing and if he didn't find his way out soon, he'd probably die.

A spark appeared in the air in front of his face and danced around him, filling him with warmth and flitting around his head. A voice whispered in his ear, "The sword will be yours, but first you must prove you are worthy of it."

"How? How can I prove I'm worthy?" Malcolm searched the cavern. Perhaps the owner of the voice was hidden in some crevice of the cave that he couldn't see.

"First, I will release you from this prison, and then you will do my bidding. When you have completed all of the tasks I've set before you, then and only then will you be able to possess the sword."

Malcolm couldn't believe it. The sword was right in front of him. He should be able to touch it and if he could touch it, he should be able to take it.

"I can hear your thoughts, Malcolm Granger. To touch the sword without first proving your worth would mean certain death."

"Who are you? Where are you?" Malcolm once again peered into every corner in search of the man who spoke to him.

"I am the one who created the sword. I am here with you and yet far away. You cannot see me or know me. You must merely do as I tell you."

Malcolm had always been at the top of his world. Never having to answer to anyone, but he wanted this sword more than anything and he was determined to have it, no matter the cost. "I'll do as you ask, within reason, of course."

"Reason should not be a problem for a ruthless man like you, Malcolm."

"Do you know me?" Most people would balk at being called ruthless, but for Malcolm it was a badge of honor.

"I have known of you ever since you discovered the existence of the sword. Your desire to own it has been transmitted to me through time and space. I have watched you and seen the kind of man you are and I know what you are capable of."

"I'm happy to know that you find me worthy of the sword." Malcolm proudly puffed out his chest.

"Worthy is not a word I'd use to describe you, Malcolm Granger, but you will certainly do."

Malcolm felt a bit of disrespect coming from this icy voice. "If I'm not worthy, then why me?" He had to control his irritation. He didn't want to anger whoever this was.

"Because you are the only one capable of breaking it free from its current resting place."

"Why won't you tell me who you are?" Malcolm rose from his spot in front of the sword and paced like a caged animal, agitated at the situation he found himself in.

"I am a powerful sorcerer, which is all you may know. My name is not to be uttered by a living soul. Each time it is, it diminishes my power and as a man of power in your own world, I'm sure you understand."

"Yes, of course." Malcolm stood up straight and tall. At least whoever this sorcerer was knew him for what he was, a powerful, successful man in his own time. "What do you need me to do?" He'd help him. He'd do anything to own the Twin Sword.

"There is a gem - an emerald - which I must have.

You must find it and bring it back here to me. Once the gem and the sword have been reunited, I will be set free and you will have your sword."

"Set free? What do you mean?" Was this man, this sorcerer, being kept here against his will?

"I have been made a prisoner of the Elfin Queen, Anania. We had a... disagreement some many years ago. She cast a spell upon me that has left me in this place - unseen and unheard until now."

"I don't understand. If you were made a prisoner, how do you still have the ability to set me free from my stone bondage? Doesn't she know what you're doing?"

"She may or may not. It is not my concern. As for my abilities, I am capable of some things and not others.

She has left me with just enough power to affect the outside world to a certain extent, but not enough to set myself free. I believe she enjoys my torment, knowing that I cannot do more than orchestrate some minor inconveniences here and there. She is much like the woman who locked you in here with the sword, Malcolm.

Women do not deserve to be the bearers of such great power. They abuse the privilege." He spat the last words out like they were poison. "When I am free, I will see to it that Anania pays for what she has done to me." The sorcerer's voice began to shake with anger and he took a moment before he spoke again. "My only wish is to be released from this prison. As I've said, Malcolm Granger, you are the only one who can help me. And as I need your help, so will you need the help of another. I have sent someone to assist you in finding the emerald."

Malcolm was beyond caring at this point. He just wanted to get his hands on that sword, but he wasn't able to break through the invisible barrier protecting it. Unfortunately, that meant he'd have to do the bidding of this *sorcerer*, the one whose name he didn't even know. This was the most ridiculous situation he could have found himself in and now he was being told he had a helper. Was he supposed to share the sword with them when he was allowed to have it?

"And exactly where is this helper and how am I supposed to find them?"

"You're a resourceful man. I have every faith that you will find them and if you should fail, then you were not meant to possess the sword."

"I'll find them, you don't have to worry about that, but are you going to give me a clue as to who or where they might be."

"That much I can do for you. *She* is at Dunaill, a castle at Dunnet Head, which is northwest of here."

"And how do you expect me to get there?" Malcolm's patience was wearing thin. He wanted to get started as soon as possible and the sorcerer was feeding him information piecemeal.

"That is your problem to deal with. You can always walk. It is a good distance from here, so it may take you some time."

"What exactly am I to do when I find this helper?" Malcolm growled.

"Mind your temper, Granger," the sorcerer snapped. "She'll lead you to the emerald I require, of course."

"Then what?" Malcolm couldn't hide his irritation with the lack of information he was receiving.

"Let's see if you're successful first and then we'll speak again." There was a cracking sound off to his left and as he turned to see what had caused it, the sorcerer said, "Now, I've created a narrow passage for you and if you head further back through it you'll find there's a small opening. I do hope you can fit through it," the sorcerer laughed heartily at this.

Malcolm on the other hand, didn't find it at all amusing. If this sorcerer needed his help, you would think he'd make it easier for him, but he knew it would do him no good to argue, because he had no idea what this sorcerer was capable of. "How will I get in touch with you?"

"I will get in touch with you. Now be off." The glow from the sword began to waiver and Malcolm used what little light it emitted to find the narrow passageway that led through to the back of the cave. It was barely wide enough for him to squeeze through, but he did his best to slither along the walls, ducking occasionally when the ceiling became too low. Eventually, he came to a much larger cavern and he was able to stand to his full height. He'd felt a tad claustrophobic as he made his way through the narrow passageway, but now he had room to breathe and he could see light filtering into this space from above.

"Damn it!" he swore. He was going to have to climb the rock walls in order to make his way out. Desperation was driving him. He couldn't stay in here much longer without food or water and, more importantly, he wanted the sword. He began to climb. It was easy at first and then became more and more difficult the higher he climbed. Hand and foot holds were difficult to see and he slipped on more than one occasion, luckily catching himself before he plummeted back to the cave floor. Time passed slowly as he searched the rock walls for a path to the top. Inch by inch he made his way until finally he could feel the cool air hitting his face from the narrow opening at the top. He only had a few more feet to go. Being extra cautious, Malcolm made it to the top but was dismayed to find the exit much smaller than it seemed from down below. Luckily there was a ledge wide enough for him to stand on, and the rock opening began to break apart as he clawed at it with his bleeding fingers. Bit by bit, the opening grew until it was just wide enough for Malcolm's large frame to pass through. He was in good shape, which was helpful because now he had to use the same bloody fingers to grasp the rock and pull his entire body weight up and through the opening. Success.

He finally made it and as he sat atop the rock formation, he could see for miles in every direction; but which way was northwest? He looked to the sky for guidance, but it must have been around noon, because the sun was directly overhead. He'd have to wait to see which direction it was headed in before he began his journey to Dunnet Head. Malcolm took the time to gather his strength. He was going to need it, because at this point he had no horse and his clothes were torn and ragged from being encased in stone and from climbing out of the cave. He'd begin his walk with the purpose of finding clothing and a horse. How he was going to do that, he had no idea.

The sorcerer told him his helper was a woman. Great! That was all he needed, some woman getting in his way.

Malcolm had always been a misogynist. He couldn't help it. Women did nothing but complicate things and he found their constant whining and complaining almost unbearable. They were little or no help as far as he was concerned. The women who worked for him did their jobs well, but he rarely gave them anything he considered executive level work. That he left to the men in his employ. This must be a test of some kind. If so, he'd pass with flying colors, even if he had to carry this woman on his back all the way back to that cave. He always came out on top and he intended to this time as well.

Malcolm had trekked many miles and from the look of things, he had many more to go. He hoped he'd find someone nearby to give him some food and perhaps a horse. As he traversed the path heading towards his helper, he heard the distinct sound of a rider coming his way. Malcolm still had his sword; no one had thought to take it away from him before he was encased in stone, so he was at least armed. As the rider approached, Malcolm made a split second decision. He would rob this man of his horse and anything else he could use.

Malcolm stood his ground in the center of the road, waving slowly to let the rider know he was in need of help. As he'd hoped, the horse went from a ground eating trot to a more leisurely walk before it stopped altogether about a foot or two away from him.

"Good sir," Malcolm faked a Scottish accent. "I need yer help. Me lady has fallen ill and I've need of help to move her to a more comfortable spot where I can set up camp."

The man skeptically looked around him and when he saw nothing, his suspicious eyes narrowed. "I dinnae see anyone."

"She's just beyond those trees." Malcolm pointed off into a heavily wooded area.

"Why dinnae ye set up yer camp there then? Nae need to move the lass."

"I suppose that I could, but I'd like to take her to a spot where she may receive more sunshine and warmth.

Please, sir, I beg of ye."

"What sickness does she have?" He seemed to be debating whether or not to help.

Malcolm understood that contagious illness would probably send the man on his way without further ado. "She's pregnant sir and I'm afeared if we dinnae stop soon, she'll have our bairn right here." He impressed even himself with his acting abilities.

The man didn't move. He sat atop his horse, obviously weighing his decision. Finally, after a long, silent wait, he said, "Verra well then, I'll help ye, but I must be on me way quickly." He dismounted and followed Malcolm off the roadside, where he found a sword at his throat and a stranger who had gone from desperate to sinister within a few steps of the road.

"I'll take yer clothes and yer horse, sir. I'm afraid I have a much greater need of them at this moment than ye."

The man stood his ground. It was obvious he did not plan on giving Malcolm anything, so Malcolm backed him into a tree, still holding the sword at his throat. "I'll kill ye as look at ye. Do as I've asked and do it quickly."

The man hesitated again and this time, Malcolm poked his neck ever so slightly with his sword, drawing blood. "Next time, ye'll be dead."

The man began disrobing and as he did, Malcolm gathered his clothes, wrapping them all within the man's cape. Forcing the man to sit at the base of a tree, he ripped some fabric from his own shirt and used it to bind the man's hands around the tree. It wasn't the best job he'd ever done of securing a knot, but it would last long enough for him to get away. Once out of sight, he'd change clothes and continue on his way to Dunnet Head.

6

Nick's excitement at nearing his home was palpable. "We're almost there, lass. 'Tis just beyond those hills." He pointed to some green and rocky hills not too far ahead of them. "Once we crest them, we'll be there." He urged his horse forward into a canter and held tightly to Katriona, lest she fall. He felt her muscles tighten and reassured her, "Ye'll be safe here and once we've gotten settled and I've had time to visit with my family, we'll see about getting ye back to Edinburgh."

He could feel her relax. "Thank you again, for coming to my aid. I'm not sure what would have happened to me if I hadn't run into you."

"'Tis best not to think on it. I fear Laird Calhoun's men would have eventually found ye and brought ye back to him. The good news is that here with my family ye will come to no harm. As fer yer marriage, ye may need to petition the church to annul it fer ye. They would surely agree, being that ye were a bride purchased against yer will."

"I hope so." She drew the cape more tightly around herself.

"Are ye still cold, lass?" The urge to protect Katriona from anything that might cause her a moment's discomfort was so strong it gave him pause. He had always been a man of honor and would do the same for anyone he told himself.

"I'm afraid I am. I've never done well in the cold and I've been so cold these last few days that I don't believe I'll thaw out for at least a week."

"If ye like, I can let ye down and ye can run alongside. That should warm ye up quickly," he teased.

"No thanks, I think I'll stay where I am. I like it here." She smiled sweetly at him, seemingly not the least put off by his odd sense of humor.

"All right then, I guess I'll just have to grit my teeth and bear it." He was continuing to tease her, but he was happy to know she wanted to stay securely in his arms. The satisfaction he received from that small acknowledgement was immense and he felt a twinge of guilt that he was enjoying it so much.

He slowed his horse to a walk, as they were approaching the hillside, which was littered with rocks of all sizes. He allowed the horse to carefully pick his way to the top and then down the other side.

His heart soared at the sight of his family castle nestled here on the cliffs of Dunnet Head, and he spurred his horse into a gallop for the last short leg of their journey. As they drew closer, voices called a warning from atop the battlements and Nick remembered that in their eyes he was either dead or long lost. He stopped short of the gate and shielding his eyes from the sun, gazed up to the top of the battlements.

"Saints be praised. I cannae believe me eyes. Is it ye, Sir Nicholas or some wily imposter come to invade our castle?" The man peering over the battlements had a wide grin on his face as he waved wildly in their direction.

"'Tis I, Alan, I see ye havenae forgotten me!" Nick called, delighted to see one of his men after all this time.

"How could we possibly forget ye, Sir Nick? We thought ye dead after all this time. Open the gates, Harry!" Alan called to someone out of their sight.

The gates creaked open and Nick and Katriona rode through to be greeted by Alan who'd run down to meet them. "Harry, go tell everyone Sir Nicholas has returned to us."

Harry ran through the courtyard, shouting at the top of his lungs, "Sir Nick is back! Sir Nick is back!"

Nick hopped down from his horse and reached up to help Katriona down. His joy at being home could hardly be contained.

Kat was captivated by the scene playing out in front of her. She wasn't sure exactly why Nick had been absent for so long. Surprisingly, they hadn't discussed it on their journey to Dunaill, but it was obvious that he'd been greatly missed. A mass of people were running towards them, all calling out excitedly to him. He was surrounded by people hugging him and patting him on the back. Kat was pushed further and further away from him as they all crowded around.

"Nick! Nick!" The crowd parted and a group of people who were obviously his family came running towards him. A woman, possibly his mother, began to cry as she spied him and ran into his arms.

"Ma," Nick choked out, obviously overcome with emotion. He held her tightly, "I dinnae wish to let ye go. I've missed ye so."

"Where have ye been, son? I've thought of ye every day since ye've been gone." She wiped her tear-filled eyes on her sleeve.

"'Tis a long story, and I'll be happy to tell ye all about it, but first I want to say hello to everyone." Kat watched as Nick reluctantly let his mother go and turned to what she assumed were his brothers and sisters. The men were beaming and the women sniffling. "I've longed to see ye all. I'm so happy to be home."

"'Tis good yer back, brother. Ye've been missed. We thought we'd lost ye fer good," the brother closest to Nick said, as he wrapped him in a bear hug. The crowd started moving towards the doors of the castle and Kat found herself being left behind. She trailed along after them not sure what to do, when Nick, who along with his brothers was at least a head taller than all the rest, turned in her direction. "Katriona, join us. Make room," he called to those around him and she found a path opened for her directly to him. "This is Katriona Hughes." Nick introduced her to everyone. "She is in need of our help and that is another story we'll share with ye."

Smiling faces greeted her and she felt the arms of Nick's mother wrap around her in a hug. "We're pleased to meet ye, Katriona. Welcome to our home. I'm Lettice, Nick's Ma. You can call me Lettie."

"Thank you. I'm happy to be here and happy to meet you." Although she was feeling a bit overwhelmed, she felt the warmth directed towards her and she smiled brightly. Perhaps she would be safe here with Nick's family.

Lettie Mackall took her hand and drew her alongside of the family. "If my Nick has brought ye home with him, ye'll be welcomed as part of the family."

Kat wasn't sure how to respond to that. Did they think she was with him in a love kind of way, or did they understand she was only here because he had rescued her? Either way, she'd set them straight after she'd had a chance to get to know them and tell them her story.

Speaking of which, could she tell them her true story, or would she be forced to continue the lie she'd created for Nick. It was probably best to go with the latter. No one here would ever believe she'd come from the future. That would cause her nothing but trouble and here in this strange place surrounded by unfamiliar people, it could be a death sentence for her.

Nick's mother led her inside to the home of the Mackalls. She wasn't quite sure what to expect, perhaps she thought it would be just like Laird Calhoun's castle - cold, sparsely furnished and completely uninviting. And so, she was completely taken aback at the warmth of this large stone fortress. She could see that everything had been done to create a homey atmosphere - rugs, tapestries, intricately carved furniture. She couldn't help but stare in complete awe at what she was seeing.

As part of her job, she spent much time on archeological sites where she was required to authenticate artifacts found there. This was a complete treasure trove of authentic medieval craftsmanship. It was five hundred years old, but in this time everything was fairly new.

There were some things that had obviously been here for a long time, but still relatively speaking, they were not artifacts. They were just everyday items that made life bearable here in this time.

"What do ye think, lass?" Nick put an arm around her shoulder. "This is my home. How I've missed it." Nick took in a deep breath, as if savoring the familiar smells of his home.

"Why were you away for so long? You never told me." Katriona was curious to hear his story and she gazed up at him expectantly.

"You'll hear soon enough. Me mother is planning a huge feast to welcome me home and I'll surely be called upon to tell everyone my tale." Eyeing him curiously, Kat couldn't help but think he seemed a bit nervous about that. Based on the man she'd gotten to know in the past few days, she didn't think public speaking something that would be difficult for him. What could it be?

"Nick, are ye going to introduce us to yer lady fair," Rory asked.

Nick laughed. "She's not my lady, but she is quite fair. This is Katriona Hughes. Katriona these be me brothers, Rory, Duncan, Lockie and Aidan." They were a handsome bunch, but none were quite as handsome as Nicholas Mackall. At least not in her opinion.

Kat greeted the group of smiling highlanders, "I'm please to meet you."

"As are we." Rory spoke for the brothers. "Welcome to Dunaill. I can see by yer face that yer entranced by our home."

"I am. It's very beautiful."

"I'd be happy to show ye the rest of it, if ye'd like." Rory had taken her by the hand and his smile had changed from the welcoming one of a few moments ago to a flirtier smile.

"I can do that, Rory. No need to trouble yerself."

Nick made it clear that Rory should back off.

"'Tis no trouble at all, brother. Ye must be tired from yer long journey and 'tis clear Katriona has an appreciation of beautiful things."

Kat could see a sibling rivalry taking place. "Maybe later, Rory. I'm quite tired myself."

"Later then. Perhaps ye'd like to come sit by the fire with..." Rory hesitated as Nick glared in his direction. "I'll leave ye then. Ye appear to be in quite capable hands."

Kat smiled in amusement at the two brothers. Nick possessively placed his hand at the small of her back to guide her through the now crowded room to a seat near the fire. "Are ye still cold, lass?"

She nodded and rubbed her arms to warm herself. "I'll get ye something to fix that." Nick moved away from her and she felt suddenly quite alone in this room full of strangers. His presence had become a comfort to her and she watched as he made his way through the crowd and then returned back to her with an oddly shaped wooden cup in hand. "Here ye are. Drink this. 'Twill help."

She put the cup to her lips, expecting tea and was surprised as a fiery liquid hit her mouth and then her throat, causing her to cough and sputter.

Nick laughed. "I'm sorry. Mayhap I should have warned ye of what ye were about to drink. I thought ye'd ken it was whiskey being as it's in a quaich."

"It's all right," she croaked out. "I was just surprised is all. Once I got past the initial taste, it felt good on the way down." She smiled up at him to let him know she was fine. "You called it a quake? Is that right?"

Nick looked confused. "Aye. A quaich, for drinking whiskey. Do ye nae drink whiskey, lass?"

Kat shook her head. "Go visit with your friends and family. I'm fine here." She didn't want to raise suspicions about where she might really be from.

"I won't be long, lass." Nick left her and headed to a group of men who immediately engulfed him in hugs and pats on the back. The sounds of their voices as they happily greeted Nick were a balm to her shattered spirit. These were the first happy people she'd met since she arrived in this time. The people at Laird Calhoun's castle never smiled.

They cowered whenever they were around their laird. She couldn't imagine living such a miserable life and was reminded why she could not be caught and returned to him. While her life had not been ideal in the twenty-first century, it had certainly been happier than what she'd experienced at the hands of Bearach Calhoun. The thought of it had her clutching her cup so tightly that her knuckles turned white. She realized she was no longer alone. Her gaze came up to meet Nick's mother and sisters.

"Are ye well, dear. Yer face is nae a happy one." Lettice Mackall observed.

"I'm fine, really. Just tired and cold." She hoped that would suffice.

"Come. We'll show ye to yer chambers and we'll get ye a nice warm bath. That should help." Nick's mother took her by the hand and pulled her up from her seat. "I don't think ye've met my daughters yet. This is Isla and this is Merry. The young women were lovely, both with long dark hair and those same tawny-colored eyes that Nick possessed. The Mackalls were a beautiful bunch. She hadn't heard word of Nick's father, so she assumed he was either not present or he had passed away. Kat didn't feel it was her place to ask, so she kept that question to herself.

They left the great hall and headed down a passageway that led them to a narrow spiral stairway. The family chambers are up these stairs," Lettie explained, leading the way.

Real medieval stairs, in a real medieval castle.

They weren't in a crumbling building, unsafe to climb and they weren't being dug up from beneath the earth. Her hands ran over the walls as she climbed, thinking of all the things she had learned about medieval castles and all the things she could learn while she was here.

The stairs curved in a clockwise direction for protection during a battle that might be waged on the stairs. The person above had the upper hand, as the attacking forces were typically right handed and at a disadvantage when attacking from below. Of course, there were always exceptions to this rule, but this castle was true to form in that regard. She was going to drink in this experience and bring it back to her own time, if she ever got there. The more she knew the better her chances of actually leading an archeological dig. She would drink it all in, everything from armor and fighting equipment to pottery and furniture. As they reached the landing, Lettie pointed to a door at the far end of the hall and to the right. That will be yer chambers, dear. They passed other doors and Kat assumed they belonged to other members of the family. As they reached the door, Kat noted another stairway going up to the next level.

"Where is Nick's room?" she asked and then realized that may not have been the best question.

His mother gave her a knowing glance and his sisters giggled. "He's across the hall from ye." She pointed to a door opposite hers.

"Oh…" She wasn't sure what to say now that she had suitably embarrassed herself.

Nick's sister opened the door for her and she entered a lovely room with a canopied bed, a fireplace, and two small windows that were shuttered against the cold. Heavy drapes fell from the ceiling and could be drawn over the windows for added protection from the cold. There was a lovely carved wooden bench at the foot of the bed and some chairs and a small table near the windows. The room was cold. It was a guest room after all and probably not in use most of the time. The girls got a fire started and the room warmed quickly. There was a knock at the door and an oblong tub was brought in and set in front of the fire.

"The water should be along shortly. Do ye have any other clothes to wear?" Lettie gazed at the torn and dirty dress Kat was wearing and shook her head. "Ye'll need something a bit more presentable. I'm sure between the three of us," she waved at the girls with her outstretched hand, "we should be able to come up with something for ye, but first we'll get ye situated in the bath."

There was another knock at the door and a string of servants carried in large buckets of steaming water, which they placed in the tub. The last girl carried some towels unlike any Kat had ever seen. She wasn't sure how good they'd be at drying her off, but there weren't any of the big fluffy kind she kept at home, so she'd have to go with these. The girl put them down on the bench and Kat noted there was a bar of soap, the sweet scent of which carried across the room. Were those roses she smelled?

The ladies wasted no time at all in removing her clothes. Kat was doing her best to keep them on, she'd never taken a bath in front of a group of women before and she was quite embarrassed. They, however, didn't seem fazed in the least by her modesty. As they removed the last bits of her clothing, all three seemed to notice her bruises at the same time. Isla covered her mouth, while Merry gasped at the sight of them.

"Who did that to ye, lass?" Lettie asked. "I hope they're no longer alive to tell the tale." She reached her hand out and touched the obvious finger marks around Kat's throat.

"My husband," Kat whispered, remembering the horrid scene on her wedding night. "Unfortunately, he's still alive and he's searching for me."

"Well, yer safe here. We'll nae allow the brute to get to ye. Let's get ye in the tub before ye freeze."

"Don't you want to know what happened?" Kat couldn't believe they weren't peppering her with questions.

"Ye can tell us if ye like, but I understand if 'tis too painful for ye to speak of." She took Kat's hand as she helped her step into the tub.

"Mmm… that feels so wonderful," Kat sank deeply into the tub, the water covering her completely. She did her best to make herself even smaller so that the water came up to her chin. She closed her eyes and smiled as she lay her head back against the tub.

The Mackalls didn't appear to be leaving. The sisters sat in the chairs and Lettie Mackall got the soap and a cloth and began to gently rub the dirt from Kat's skin.

"You don't have to go to all that trouble," Kat said, again feeling embarrassed. "I can do it."

"Nae. Ye rest yerself. 'Tis nothing I wouldnae do fer any of my lot." She brushed the cloth across Kat's shoulders, being careful not to press too hard on her bruises, but managing to get her clean just the same.

Kat resigned herself to the fact that she was being treated as she would expect the queen to be treated by this lovely family. They were all being so kind to her, something she wasn't used to even in her life in the future. It felt odd, but she tried to let go of that and just be grateful they were so kind.

Once Lettie got her body all cleaned, she started in on Kat's hair. Yer hair is such a lovely golden color dear. Once we get all the dust and dirt out of it, it will shine like the sun. She vigorously scrubbed Kat's scalp, which felt wonderful to her and when she was done, she rinsed all the soap out.

"Would ye like to stay in there longer, I think the water is cooling quickly and we don't want ye to get a chill." She tipped her head around to see Kat's reaction.

"I'll get out now, thank you." Kat stood and was immediately enveloped in a large drying cloth. The women vigorously rubbed her arms and legs, making Kat uncomfortable with their fussing over her.

"Thank you for your help, but there's really no need. I can dry myself." She didn't want to sound ungrateful, but she had never been one who appreciated people fussing over her. When she was a child, she always wanted to do everything herself. From picking her own outfits to brushing her hair, Kat was very independent even during her childhood.

"Isla please go see what dresses ye can find fer Katriona to wear. She looks to be about yer size." And then to Kat, "I'll have this one cleaned fer ye."

For some inexplicable reason, tears stung at Kat's eyes and she rubbed them away with the back of her hand.

"Why are ye crying, lass? We're not here to harm ye." Lettie rubbed Kat's shoulder to comfort her.

"I'm sorry. I know you won't hurt me. I don't really know why I'm crying. I was just overcome with emotion.

Please excuse me."

"There's nothing to excuse. Ye've been through a horrible ordeal and now that yer here and safe, I imagine it's the first time ye've had a chance to allow yerself to feel."

Kat was astonished at how perceptive Lettie was. She and the sisters continued to tut-tut over her.

Isla left the room in search of clothing for Kat and the other two women cleaned up around the tub. Wiping water off of the floor and placing the soap on the tray it came on.

A knock at the door sent three heads flying up to glance in the direction of the entryway. "Who's there?" Lettie asked.

"Nick," was the reply. "Is Katriona with ye? I didn't see her downstairs and I worried."

"Yes, dear, she's here. We're getting her cleaned up and finding some clothes for her to wear. She's fine.

We'll be back down soon."

"I'll see ye in the great hall, Kat," Nick called through the door.

Kat didn't know what to say to that, so she said nothing. Nick must have waited by the door for her reply and when he heard none, she noted the sound of his receding footsteps as he made his way back to the stairs. "You must all be so happy to have Nick back home. He told me he's been gone for two years."

"Aye. It's been a sad time here without him. He's the eldest and to be laird, ye ken. We thought him dead. 'Twas a shock to see him in the courtyard, but a good shock. My heart is singing happily at his return."

Kat felt guilty for keeping her from her son. "Lettie, you should be with Nick and not up here with me. Really, I can take care of myself. I can imagine ye'll have many questions for him."

"Aye. I will. But 'tis here I wish to be. We'll get ye dressed and we'll be with him in no time, ye'll see."

7

Nick was concerned when he hadn't seen Katriona seated where he'd left her. He hoped she hadn't decided to run away again. That would be a very poor choice on her part. Somehow he didn't think she would, but he had decided to head upstairs to the guest chambers to see if she was there.

A smile lit his lips at the sound of his mother's voice telling him everything was fine and they were helping her bathe. He hoped Katriona was enjoying all the attention they were lavishing on her. He didn't know her well, but after the ordeal she'd just been through, he imagined she could use some mothering.

After heading back downstairs to join the others, Nick's thoughts kept wandering to Katriona. Laird Calhoun had best hope he never crossed paths with him, or he would be a verra sorry bastard. He deserved to receive some of the same treatment he had meted out to Katriona. Nick had always been taught to respect and care for women and he had never strayed from that. Two years in San Francisco hadn't changed him and he doubted anything ever would.

"There ye be, brother," Duncan called as Nick hit the bottom of the stairs. "Tell us of yer adventures. Where did ye go the day the three of us were hunting?"

The others had gathered around and Nick wasn't so sure he wanted to tell them the truth. They'd surely think him tetched in the head. "More whiskey," he requested, stalling for time.

"Rory, see to it," Duncan ordered. Duncan was a year younger than Nick and Rory was next. Lockie and Aidan were the last of the boys and then Isla and Merry were born. The Mackall clan kept his mother busy throughout their childhoods. Their father died shortly after the last sister was born, but Lettie Mackall managed to raise her family and keep the rest of the clan together despite the fact she was a woman, and it was unusual for anyone other than a man to be in charge. She had only handed the reins over to Nick a month before he went missing and apparently Duncan had filled the position when Nick hadn't returned.

"I was thinking I'd tell ye about it later when everyone was present, perhaps at the feast."

"Ye can tell it again. Curiosity has gotten the better of us. Tell us," Duncan urged.

Gathering his thoughts and accepting the whiskey his younger brother brought him, Nick settled himself in to tell his tale, leaning up against the fireplace mantle. Everyone in the room waited with rapt anticipation. "Well, as ye ken, we were hunting a giant of a stag.

Rory and I went our separate ways trying to flush the stag in Duncan's direction. As I crept through the woods, I came upon a bridge I didn't recall seeing before and a strange blanket of fog which swirled only in one spot, blocking the entrance to the bridge." He glanced around him to see if he had everyone's attention and once he was certain he did, he continued. "The fog was of an unusual sort. I walked nearer and couldn't help myself. It was as if I were being pulled closer and closer. Eventually I found myself inside of the fog, which was filled with lights of different colors."

"Were ye afeared," old Garbhan asked from his seat by the fire.

"Nay, I wasnae." Nick decided to tell his version of the truth. It would be more acceptable to those around him who believed in faeries and the wee folk. "I kept walking, unable to see where I was headed. When I finally came out on the other side of the fog, I was in a wondrous place. 'Twas like nothing I'd ever seen. I tried to hide, but eventually they found me."

"Who found ye, Nick?" Lockie asked, his eyes wide with the wonder of it all.

"The faeries!" Nick glanced around the room, making sure everyone was still with him. "They live in a wondrous land. 'Tis filled with things the likes of which ye've never seen."

"What did they do when they found ye? Did they make ye their prisoner?" Aidan was on the edge of his seat.

"Nae. I told them I must return home, but they said it would nae be possible unless I helped them. Ye see they were expecting a battle to occur and they needed my help to teach them how to fight their foes. I wasnae so sure I wanted to do that, but I did want to come home, so I agreed. I worked with them each and every day for quite a long time. At first, they battled their foes, but lost. They needed more work, so I put them through their paces for many months. They fed me and clothed me and gave me a palace to live in all my own. Deciding I needed help, they enticed another from our world to join me and the two of us were better able to lead the faeries in their battle."

"Did ye win?"

"Aye! We did! It was an easy victory and the faeries were so happy that they wanted me to stay with them forever. I reminded them of our bargain and being bound by their own words, they allowed me to come home. And so here I am." Nick hoped his far-fetched story would suffice. It was true to a certain extent with the exception of the faeries. He omitted the fact that he had time-travelled. Why it was easier for them to accept his tale of the faeries than it was to accept a tale of time-travel, he wasn't sure. They were familiar with faeries and time-travel was not something he recalled ever hearing about in their folklore. "And now I have one question for me brothers? Did ye get the stag?"

"We did," Duncan said. "Although the joy at catching it was short-lived when we realized that you were no longer anywhere to be found. We came home and told Ma that ye'd disappeared. She made us go right back to the place we'd last seen ye to search for ye and we did.

Rory, Lockie, Aidan and I all spent many days and nights tirelessly searching, but eventually we gave up. When you rode through the gates today, it was as if in answer to our prayers. We had given up on ever seeing you again and yet, here ye be."

"And here I plan to stay." Nick breathed deeply the familiar scents of his hearth and home. "What of Skye? Did she ever marry?" He hoped she had. The lass surely wouldnae have waited two years for his return.

"Nay, but she is to wed and soon. Yer being back may change that. Her father wished her to marry ye."

"Does she love this man she's to marry?"

"Aye. She is verra much in love with him and he with her as I've heard. 'Twill be a shame if she cannae marry the man."

"Well, we'll need to be sure she can. I've no wish to marry the lass. Truth be told, I didnae wish to marry her before I disappeared to live with the faeries. I only agreed to it because it was good for our clan to be allied with the Maguires ye ken. I'd prefer to marry for love, as our Ma and Da did."

Kat waited beside the entry to the great hall, listening intently to the crazy story Nick was weaving. He couldn't possibly be telling the truth, but if he wasn't, then where had he gone off to? Why would he stay away for two whole years? It couldn't possibly have been to avoid marriage. He didn't seem like the type of man who would shirk his responsibilities and she knew full well there were no faeries, so where was he? He had to have a very good reason for not telling his own family his whereabouts. It piqued her curiosity and Kat vowed to find out what the real story was.

"No need to stand out here, Katriona. Come join the others inside the great hall." Lettie hooked her arm through Kat's and led her into the hall. Kat felt much better now that she'd bathed and changed her clothes.

She felt more like her old self and perhaps even pretty, in the beautiful sage green dress she'd been given to wear and the fancy braiding Mrs. Mackall had done to her hair. Kat hesitantly stepped into the hall and was met with the stares of every man present, but none of them mattered more to her than Nick Mackall. His was the only head she wished to turn. She had no idea why, but it mattered to her that he gazed at her with admiration and a whistle on his lips.

"And who is this lovely lass?" Nick strode to her side and gave her an appraising gaze from head to toe. "Ye cannae be the lass I found in the forest on my way back home."

Kat blushed under his scrutiny and giggled at his silliness.

"Nick Mackall, dinnae tease the poor lass. She's been through a rough time." As Lettie scolded Nick, she also smiled in obvious joy at having him home.

"Sorry, Ma and I beg yer pardon, Katriona. Ye look beautiful." Nick appeared quite apologetic as he gazed down at her with eyes that sparkled with flecks of gold and bronze.

"It's okay. I know I was probably a sight when you found me racing through the trees. I feel much better now." Kat smoothed down the front of her dress to hide her awkwardness.

"I'm happy to hear it. Ye have nothing to fear here with us. Laird Calhoun willnae ken where ye've gone off to and with any luck, never will. But ken this, should he find ye, he'll have to answer to me for his poor treatment of ye, lass." From the expression on his face, Kat didn't doubt that Bearach Calhoun would find himself in a sorry state at the hands of Nick Mackall.

"Was it Laird Calhoun I jest heard ye mention?" Osgar the village innkeeper asked, eyeing Kat from the corner of his eyes.

"Aye. He's a mean bastard. He beat this poor lass after she was forced to marry him," Nick explained.

"She's his wife then?" Osgar had a strange look on his face. One that Kat found a bit disconcerting. It made her almost as uncomfortable as it did being spoken of like she wasn't even in the room.

"In name only. Kat lost her family to some highwaymen and was found by a man who gained her trust and then sold her to Calhoun to be his wife." Nick gazed at Kat with a warm smile on his lips. It was as if he was saying he understood her discomfort at all this attention.

The man shook his head in understanding and said no more, but Kat was now nervous nonetheless.

The Mackalls were a warm and loving family and to celebrate Nick's return, they planned a celebration in his honor to take place in two weeks time. Messengers were sent to the village and to their neighbors, inviting all to come for a great feast. The castle was spotlessly cleaned from top to bottom and preparations were made in the kitchen. The hall would be overflowing with ale and whiskey when the time came.

Nick made sure that Kat felt included in all the preparations. She helped Lettie and his sisters without complaint. It was as if she were a member of the family. She fit right in with them all and before long she was taking part in the good natured teasing that the Mackalls enjoyed with each other. Nick couldn't seem to stop himself from glancing in her direction whenever she was nearby and he also couldn't help but seek her company when he'd gone more than a few short hours without seeing her. He felt himself growing quite fond of her and even pictured himself with her by his side, raising a family of wee ones here at Castle Dunaill.

Despite her good nature, Kat was obviously worried about the feast. "Nick, I'm afraid. What if Bearach finds out where I am and comes after me?" The quivering of her voice told Nick exactly how concerned she really was.

"That willnae happen, lass. And if by some strange chance it did, ye've the entire Mackall clan here to protect ye. Calhoun would have to come here with an entire army and even then he'd never stand a chance.

Dinnae fear, not a soul here would betray ye." He wrapped a protective arm around her shoulders and drew her in to his embrace. She went willingly, even snaking her own arms around his waist. He planted a kiss on the top of her head and then set her away from him so he could look her in the eye. "I promised ye before and I promise ye now. I'll nae allow any harm to come to ye, Kat. Do ye believe me?"

"I do." Kat nodded her head and smiled up at him.

Her emerald green eyes sparkled brightly while Nick felt himself falling under their spell.

Nick found himself spending more and more time with Kat. He sought out any time alone with her he could get, escorting her on walks around the castle whenever possible. Their connection to each other was growing. He only hoped nothing would stand in the way of him making her his.

On one of their daily walks, Kat brought up the subject of the faeries. "Nick, the other day, I heard you telling your clan about being transported to the land of the faeries." She stopped and looked up at him, gauging his response. "That can't possibly be true.

Where were you really?"

"Do ye nae believe in faeries, Katriona? I'm surprised at ye, a good Scottish lass born and raised and ye doubt their existence." Nick teased her, and Kat knew it was his way of trying to avoid the subject.

Kat laughed. "You know there's no such thing. Where were you?" There was no way she was going to give up.

"I'm afraid I cannae divulge that information, lass."

"And why not?" She tipped her head and gazed at him with mischief in her eyes.

"'Tis a secret." Nick couldn't possibly imagine that would work.

"A secret?" *Two can play this game.*

"Aye, a secret." He said it again, as if that would be the end of it.

"Are you sure you don't wish to share it with me?" "Aye. I cannae give away all my confidences now can I?" He began to walk again, but Kat put out a hand to stop him.

"You're hiding something, I can tell." She narrowed her eyes and searched his face.

"Mayhap 'tis because ye, yerself are hiding something?" He paused a moment, waiting for her to answer. "Would ye care to tell me the true story of how ye came to find yerself the prisoner and wife of Laird Calhoun?"

"I'm afraid I can't divulge that information, sir." It was Kat's turn to walk away, as Nick hurried to catch up with her.

"And why nae?" he asked.

"Because of the whole faerie thing." Kat hoped she could swing the conversation back to his secret.

"What do ye mean, blaming the faeries! What do they have to do with it?" Nick appeared confused.

"Nothing." Kat tried in vain to hide her giggle. "Nothing. Is that all ye have to say fer yerself, lass?" Nick's smile told her he was enjoying their banter.

"Aye. I can't give away all my secrets now can I?" "Ye've got me there." Nick laughed and poked her side.

Kat shrieked in mock dismay and then ran as fast as her feet would carry her. She had no idea where she was running, but at first it was fun that Nick was chasing her. He caught her fairly quickly. He did have an advantage after all. He was so tall and had those long legs. His strides were twice as long as her. He grabbed her around the waist and began to tickle her. Kat couldn't help it, but her gut reaction was to get away from him. Thoughts of the torment of her wedding night ran unbidden through her head and instead of seeing Nick, she saw Laird Calhoun. She struck out at him and Nick, looking quite shocked, grabbed her hand before the blow landed on his handsome face.

"I'm only playing with ye, lass. There's no need to strike me. Just tell me to stop and I will." Her hand was engulfed in his much larger one and he held on to it, despite the fact she tried to pull it away.

"I'm sorry." Unwanted tears made an appearance in her eyes and she gazed down at the ground to hide them from Nick. "I forgot it was you who had grabbed me."

Nick pulled her into his arms and she buried her face in his chest. "The only thing I could think of was Laird Calhoun and that I had to get away from him. I'm so sorry."

"Lass, there's nae need for apologies, although I believe I'll be needing a dry shirt when yer done with all yer crying."

This last comment made Kat giggle. She raised her tear stained face to see Nick's warm smile beaming at her. How could she possibly think that this man would ever do anything to hurt her? He was no Laird Calhoun. Could never be.

"Now, shall we continue our walk and I promise I willnae chase ye anymore?"

"Good. That means I can run away from you without worry," she teased.

"Shall we continue our walk?" Nick repeated. Kat nodded her assent.

"I've an idea. Would ye care to go to the village, perhaps an afternoon away from the castle would be to yer liking."

"I'd love that!" As soon as she said it, she began to worry. "But what if we see someone there who knows Laird Calhoun. I think I should stay here."

"Nonsense. I dinnae believe ye'll see anyone ye know at our little village. I'll be with ye and no one will bother ye. But if ye'd rather stay here than go to see the shops with me, then so be it." The serious expression on his face belied the fact that he was obviously having some fun at her expense.

"Shops!" Katriona hadn't been shopping in ages. Not since months before she accidentally found herself in the sixteenth century. She really did want to go and she could trust Nick, couldn't she? "All right. I'll go."

Nick smiled triumphantly. "I ken the way to a lassie's heart now, dinnae I?"

8

"Nick is taking me to the village to see the shops." Kat shared the news with Nick's sisters. They were total opposites, but each of them had qualities that Kat enjoyed. She hadn't had many friends growing up. She never stayed in one place for very long and the children she did come across could be quite cruel. They teased her relentlessly about being an orphan and in long term foster care. Isla and Merry knew nothing about her life before they met her and they were very welcoming. They felt like sisters, or so Kat imagined and she wondered how they'd feel if they knew the truth about her.

"I believe me brother fancies ye," Isla said. She was busy folding clothing that had been hung to dry.

"I don't think so." Kat couldn't believe Nick would be attracted to her, even though she herself was undeniably drawn to him.

"Kat, ye fancy him, dinnae ye!" Merry's eyes went wide with the realization. "Ye do. Why else would ye be turning so red?"

Kat wished there was a hole she could crawl into.

This was not a subject she wished to discuss with Nick's sisters.

"Leave her be, Merry. Cannae ye see she doesnae wish to speak of it." Isla finished the folding and took Kat's hand. "No matter what ye think ye ken, lass, I know me brother. I can see the way his eyes follow you around the room and the way he smiles when yer near him.

Kat wished with all her heart for it to be true, but how could it be? They'd only known each other a brief time and had met under the most unfortunate of circumstances. His only interest was in protecting her, and her only interest was in returning to her own time. She couldn't possibly get involved with Nick, but was it already too late.

It was market day and the village was bustling with people shopping for essentials and just out to visit with each other. This was a social event for most and they wouldn't miss it for the world. Nick guided Kat through the center of the village and they made a few stops at shops selling all sorts of finery. He could see Katriona was mesmerized by it all and decided then and there that he would purchase a small trinket or two in remembrance of their day together. Their first stop was a dress shop. Nick was enjoying the look of wonder on Kat's face as she held first one and then another of the dresses up to herself.

"Oh, this one's beautiful," she gushed as she spun around with the dress in her arms. Nick surreptitiously nodded to the shop keeper who nodded back in unspoken acknowledgment of the message being passed between the two. As soon as Kat put the dress down, the shopkeeper took it from her and made a show of placing it back where she'd found it, but in fact as soon as they left the shop he would set it aside for Nick. They also stopped in a fabric shop and at a jeweler. She saw something she liked in both places and as in the dress shop, when she wasn't looking, Nick had words with the shopkeepers and they set aside the items she seemed the most drawn to. He would have them delivered to Dunaill and surprise her with them.

After leaving the jewelers, they headed towards the inn. Nick thought it a good idea to buy her some food and to sit and relax with her by his side.

"Are ye hungry, Kat?" He thought he knew the answer.

He'd heard her stomach grumbling a few times as they shopped.

"Very. Can we get something to eat?" She gazed at him with such innocence he wished he could take the whole day to just enjoy her lovely face.

"Aye. This way." Nick led her to the door of the inn, opening it for her to enter. They hadn't taken two steps in when Nick noted two familiar faces peering across the room at them, one was shocked and the other quite angry.

"Is that Nick Mackall I see?" the portly gentleman asked, sounding none too pleased.

Nick hesitated only momentarily. "Aye. 'Tis I."

"Do ye see that, me love?" the man said to the young woman who sat beside him. "Yer Nick has come back fer ye."

Kat bristled at this announcement. Was this Nick's bride-to-be? She had an unexpected rush of jealousy as she gazed on the dark-haired beauty who appeared quite uneasy on seeing them.

"Father, I dinnae believe he came back for me." Skye Maguire protested perhaps a little too loudly. "I dinnae wish to marry Nick Mackall. I wish to marry Taran." She stood and glared at both men, her eyes welling with tears.

"My dear, dinnae argue with me. Ye shall marry Nick as was the plan before his odd disappearance. Isn't that right, Nick?" Skye's father raised his voice to match his daughter's, not caring that he created a disturbance. Others in the dining room turned to stare. It seemed they would have a show along with their meal.

"Sir, I'm afraid I cannae marry yer daughter. She doesnae wish to marry me and I…"

"Is there some problem, husband?" Katriona asked, interrupting Nick's attempt at reasoning with Maguire.

Nick tried not to act surprised by this. He raised an eyebrow in her direction. "No, my love. None."

"Are ye married then?" Domhnall Maguire rose from his chair, as had his daughter. He was sputtering and fuming, growing redder by the moment, obviously not able to believe what he was hearing.

"Aye, so it would seem. While I was away, I met this lovely lass, and as it had been so long since I'd seen yer daughter, I assumed Skye would have married. What can I say? We fell in love and I've been living in her village. I wasnae sure I would ever get back here." Nick placed a possessive arm around Kat's waist. He was no fool; he'd take full advantage of the situation that had been presented to him.

"My daughter was promised to ye. Ye've broken our contract. I cannae believe ye'd go and betray me… her!" Domhnall shouted.

"Father, please sit." Skye placed a hand on his arm and did her best to guide him back into his seat.

"My apologies. 'Twas nae my intention to betray anyone. And now if ye'll excuse us, we've need of some food and drink. 'Twas a pleasure seeing you again, Domhnall. Skye." He bowed in their direction and then taking Katriona by the hand, led her to a back corner table far away from any further confrontation with the Maguire.

"I'm sorry, I hope I didn't make things worse. I was just trying to help." Katriona tipped her head and gazed sweetly up at him.

"All is well, Katriona. Thank ye fer coming to me rescue. I had no intentions of marrying her, especially now that I ken she is in love. I would have her be happy in her marriage and I would be happy in mine."

"Do you think he believed us?" Kat glanced over to Skye's table.

"I hope so." He brought her hand to his lips, brushing a soft kiss across her knuckles and gazing sweetly into her eyes. He noted that Domhnall was staring at him and he did his best to be convincing, although it wasnae difficult to appear smitten with Kat. He'd be sure to let the family know what had transpired, so as to avoid any misunderstandings at future meetings with the Maguires."

A serving girl arrived at their table with a pitcher of ale and two cups. "Sir Nick. 'Tis good to see ye again. I'd heard ye were back."

"Aye. Good news and gossip travel quickly," he teased.

She batted at his shoulder. "Yer still the funny one, arenae ye?"

"Could ye bring us some food, whatever ye've got today is fine."

"Me Ma made her famous stew. I'll bring two bowls and some freshly baked bread. By the way, me name's Shona," she said to Katriona.

"Katriona," Kat said in answer.

"I should tell ye, Katriona is me wife," Nick added, noting Katriona's blush.

"Are ye now?" The girl smiled widely at her. "I never thought I'd see the day when Nick Mackall took a wife. Rumor has it that the reason ye disappeared was to avoid that one." She waved her hand in the direction of Domhnall and Skye.

"Well I'm happy to ken that I've kept the rumor mongers busy in my absence. I'm back now and I've brought me wife with me. We are verra happy. Arenae we, me love?" He looked lovingly into Katriona's eyes.

"Aye. Very happy." He could almost believe it, she was that convincing.

"Happy I am fer ye." Shona made a show of tidying up the table. "How be yer brother?" she asked.

"Which one?" Nick winked at her, causing her to wrinkle her brow at his question.

"Ye ken which one. I've nay seen him in the village of late." Shona said. She appeared to be doing her best to sound like she didn't care one way or the other.

"Duncan has been busy taking care of things at Dunaill. Ye ken while I was away he was the laird." Nick knew his brother was quite taken with Shona.

"I ken it. Mayhap now that ye've returned we'll see more of him. Tell him I was asking after him." With that Shona turned and walked away.

"She likes your brother," Kat stated.

"Aye. That she does. Always has, since they were wee bairns." Nick gave Kat his undivided attention, partially because he couldn't stop staring into her mesmerizing green eyes and partially to keep up the pretense of being married to this lovely creature.

Kat, for her part, seemed to be playing along. Was she really gazing into his eyes with the longing that he saw in hers, or was it all for show? At that moment he wanted more than anything to reach across the table and cradle her face in his hands as he kissed her full rosy lips. As he gazed longingly at those lips, her tongue darted out to lick them. Damn it! Was she trying to kill him with this innocent seduction? Or did she know what she was doing to him? He thanked the heavens that there was a table between them, leaving Kat unable to see his rising kilt. Unable to resist a moment longer, he touched her soft cheek with his thumb. A sharp intake of her breath told him she felt the same jolt he was feeling.

"You two must be newly wed. Yer gaping at each other like two lovesick cows," Shona chuckled as she placed a bowl of stew in front of each of them. "I'll be back with the bread and some ale. Ye'll want to eat that stew while it's hot. Then ye can go back to ogling each other. We've got a free bed upstairs if ye cannae wait till yet get back home." She laughed out loud at that one and Nick and Kat tore their gazes away from each other to focus on the food in front of them.

Katriona sat closely by Nick's side wondering if she hadn't just made the biggest mistake of her life. Well, maybe not the biggest. That would be the mistake she'd made when she'd picked up that damn emerald at the site of Malcolm Granger's archeological dig in Southern Caithness. She'd never seen one that size before. It was beautiful, and it felt as if it were calling to her. She couldn't resist a closer look and besides, how was she to know that as soon as she placed it in the palm of her hand she'd be transported kicking and screaming to sixteenth-century Scotland, where she'd be running for her life.

This mistake was one that could hopefully be corrected as soon as she disappeared from the lives of the Mackalls and returned to her life in London. Nick seemed to be enjoying this ruse, but she wasn't so sure it would be easy to convince anyone else of their marriage, especially since there hadn't been one.

"Nick, is this going to cause a problem?" she asked, concern in her voice.

"I dinnae believe so. The only people we need to convince are those who arenae immediate members of my family. So, pretty much everyone at the castle and everyone here in the village." He chuckled at that.

"Oh… I'm sorry. I do that sometimes… speak before I think, I mean. I was only trying to help." She took another bite of her stew, which was better than she'd imagined it would be. The food she'd eaten at Calhoun's had been practically inedible and while she'd enjoyed every meal at Dunaill, she wasn't sure if it would be the case here at the inn.

"I ken that and I appreciate ye making the effort.

We'll have to make a good show of it for them, ye ken." Nick broke off a piece of bread and handed it to her.

"I do." And she did. It wouldn't be hard at all; Nick was tall, good looking and fun to be with. Hadn't she just been staring at him all googly-eyed? As long as she didn't have to sleep with him, she could pull this off no problem. Of course, the thought of sleeping with Nick didn't seem too bad. As a matter of fact, it seemed more than appealing to her, but neither one of them was in need of more problems in their lives. He was her friend and probably wasn't interested in her in that way, right? Of course he wasn't. What had just happened between them was all for the benefit of the others dining at the inn. No. She would be sure to keep her feelings for Nick to herself and hope that she could get back home before it became impossible to hide them.

Nick considered this to be the best problem he'd ever had in all his years on this earth. Katriona was a bonny lass and he was verra attracted to her. She, of course, was already married to Laird Calhoun and that situation needed to be taken care of before he could even consider her anything other than a friend. Hopefully she hadn't noticed how enchanted he was with her.

"We should be sure to hold hands as we walk back to the castle," Nick noted.

"Of course," Kat replied and she held out her hand for him to take.

Nick felt like a young lad as he happily took it and walked with her by his side. He couldn't have wiped the smile off his face if he tried. He was in heaven and certain parts of his body were becoming difficult to keep under control. It was a lot of work, but somehow he managed.

Finally reaching the castle, Nick gathered the family around and filled them in on what had occurred in the village.

"Yer quick on yer feet, Katriona," Isla said. "Thank ye fer saving me brother and Skye from being forced together."

"Why were you getting married in the first place if no one wanted it?" Katriona couldn't quite wrap her brain around that one. Skye was in love with another man and wished to marry him and Nick was not the marrying kind, from what Shona said about him.

"We liked each other well enough and if it came right down to it, I would have done my duty and married her, but that was before I disappeared and before I found out that she was in love with another." *And before I found you.* "I could never marry her now. I want her to be happy and she wouldnae ever be happy with me."

"Why not?" Kat tipped her head and cocked an eyebrow as she waited for her answer.

"Because she doesnae love me. She loves another." Nick thought that was obvious, but Katriona was full of questions, as usual. He loved her curiosity, and never tired of answering her questions, but these questions served no purpose and he thought she may have been trying to make him uncomfortable.

"The night of the celebration ye'll be forced to pretend that yer a married couple. That may require a bit more than standing next to each other and dancing a dance or two." Lettie gave them each an appraising eye. "Do ye think yer up to the challenge?"

"Aye. How difficult can it be to appear head over heels in love with each other?" Nick chuckled and turned to Kat. "Mayhap we should practice."

"Practice. I don't think so." She shook her head vehemently. Apparently she'd overcome the feelings he saw displayed at the inn.

"This was yer idea, remember?" He cocked an eyebrow in her direction.

"Yes, it was, but I never imagined it would go this far." She seemed uncomfortable with the direction this conversation was taking.

"'Tis too late to turn back now. Maguire has likely blabbed it to everyone in the village and then, of course, everyone at his home.

"I'm afraid yer in fer some scrutiny." Lettie said.

Kat rolled her eyes. "All right. Fine. I'll do my best to appear smitten with ye."

Nick looked suitably hurt. "Kat, I'm sorry to hear that it will be such a burden fer ye to be my wife." He snuck a peek in her direction, holding back a grin as he did.

Kat obviously wasn't about to let him get away with that one. "Yes. Well, let's hope I don't give you away, or to the altar you will march, with one very unhappy bride."

By now the rest of the family caught on to their teasing and they all groaned as they turned to leave the room. The only person who did not appear to think this was funny was old Garbhan.

"'Tis never a good thing to lie, Sir Nick. Ye'll surely be caught."

"Dinnae waste another thought on it. We willnae get caught, ye'll see." Nick patted him on the back and both he and Kat turned away and left a perplexed Garbhan in their wake.

9

Guests to the celebration began arriving days in advance and would
be staying at the castle, as it would be too far for them to travel back
home the night of the feast. Kat was delighted to know she would
have company in her chamber, as Isla and Merry Mackall had given up
theirs to those visitors who would need accommodations. Kat was
used to being on her own. She lived by herself in her tiny flat back in
London, but something about being in a different time had her fearing
the nights in this large and lonely castle. Lonely wasn't quite the right
word.

There were plenty of people around and they had been so welcoming to her. She felt as much at home here as she had felt anywhere
in her life, perhaps even more so, but she couldn't relax, no matter
how kind they'd been; she still feared Laird Calhoun would show up
on the doorstep at any moment and force her to go back home with
him.

The thought made her shiver in apprehension. She knew if that
ever happened, she might not live to tell the tale.

He had to be furious with her for trying to kill him and for running away from him, which had caused him embarrassment. She was
sure it would not end well for her, especially because she would never
submit willingly. So having someone in her room with her at night,
even for a few nights, would help. Someone to talk to about any inane
thing was better than the thoughts running through her head whenever
she found herself alone.

In the back of her head, Kat couldn't help but wish it was Nick who would be sharing her bed. She felt safe and having him there beside her, holding her in his strong arms was all she'd been able to think about since she'd arrived. This thing going on between them had gotten weird quickly after Kat blurted out that Nick was her husband. The celebration, which should have merely been a welcome home for Nick had turned into a wedding reception now because of her meddling. They would have to dutifully play the happily married couple, which shouldn't be too hard. Nick was handsome, charming and so much fun to be around. *What could possibly go wrong?* She asked herself. *Everything* was her answer. They really needed to have a game plan. She didn't want to get caught off guard and blow their cover. That would never do. She'd have to speak with Nick about it. She had absolutely no idea what to expect of married life in sixteenth-century Scotland. In her time, couples kissed in public, they held hands, they were very touchy-feely. She hadn't noticed any of that happening here, of course she hadn't really been paying attention either.

The following morning, a rider approached from the village with a large parcel thrown across the saddle in front of him.

"Katriona," Nick called to her. "Come with me, I believe this package is for ye."

"For me." She was a bit apprehensive. How could any package in this time be for her? She knew very few people here other than the Mackalls. "Are you sure?" she asked as she hesitantly made her way to Nick's side.

"Aye. Come. Hurry." He grabbed her hand and hauled her along behind him as he joyfully headed in the direction of the rider.

"Sir Nick," the rider bowed his head from atop his saddle. "I have a package here for yer lovely bride." He handed the neatly wrapped package to Nick.

"Thank ye." Nick gave him some coin and the lad turned his horse and road out through the gate.

"What is it?" Kat asked excitedly. "A wedding present?"

"Shall we go inside and see?" He grabbed Kat's hand again and this time she kept up with him easily. A package for her! Nick's excitement was contagious and she was anxious to open it.

They reached the great hall and instead of stopping, Nick led her up the stairway and down the hall to her chamber. He quickly peeked up and down the hallway and when he saw no one about, he opened the door and pulled her inside before slamming the door behind them.

"What are you doing?" Kat was surprised to find herself alone in her room with Nick. The fluttering in her belly told her she felt something more. Her thoughts and Nick's presence would surely be frowned upon by the others. "Is this a good idea?"

"Ye forget, we're married." Nick winked and smiled that mischievous smile of his.

"Not really though." She quickly glanced away so he wouldn't be able to read the wanton feelings she was having.

"I've bought ye a wedding present, Kat. Open it."

She gazed at him with a question in her eyes and he nodded at the package. Kat reached for the string, untying it in one smooth motion. The fabric wrapping fell away and there sat the lovely dress, shoes and jewels she had seen in the village. Reverently, she reached out a tentative hand to touch the silky gold fabric of the dress. "Oh, Nick. You shouldn't have!"

"And why not? I saw how much ye liked them and it was a small thing for me to do. I want ye to be as happy as possible while yer here with us, Katriona."

Without thinking, she stood on tiptoe, quickly kissing his cheek and shyly looking away, before lifting the dress out of the package and holding it up in front of her. "Do you think it will fit me?" she asked.

"Aye. The shop owner has a good eye. If it doesnae, my sisters and my mother can help ye to adjust it in any way necessary." Nick appeared to be pleased with Kat's reaction to the gift.

Picking up the topaz earrings and matching necklace, Katriona held them in her hands and stared. She'd never had anything so beautiful in her life. She could barely afford her rent and groceries with her paycheck, so jewelry was a luxury she only appreciated as she passed by the shops on her way to work and peered in their windows. "Thank you, Nick. You're very sweet to do this." She hoped he knew how grateful she truly was.

"I cannae wait to see them on ye. I believe ye'll be the most beautiful lass at the feast. A golden princess." His eyes twinkled as he watched her try on the shoes, which fit perfectly.

"I feel like Cinderella," she said. "And who might that be, lass?"

"Oh, just someone in a story I heard growing up. Her fairy godmother made her look beautiful for the ball and she met the prince and he fell in love with her and they lived happily ever after." That was embarrassing. She hoped he didn't think she meant she'd live happily ever after with him. "Of course, that's just a story. It never happens in real life."

Nick's expression was serious, his eyes examining her face in a way that was making her a little uncomfortable. "Why do ye think it never happens in real life? I've seen it happen and I believe it to be so."

"Well, I guess it can happen for some people, but they'd be few and far between." She was avoiding his eyes, which seemed to be peering right into her soul.

"Kat, ye must believe that happiness is all around ye. Ye need only seek it and ye'll find it. I promise ye. I ken ye've not had much luck of late, especially with that bastard Calhoun, but have faith."

The only happily ever after Kat wished for was to go back to her life in London. The life before she fell through time. It was unlikely that was going to happen, and if it didn't, then what? She'd be stuck here. The Mackalls wouldn't allow her to stay forever; she was sure of that based on the number of foster homes she'd been in and out of. And if her experience with the people of medieval Scotland after she'd first arrived was any indication, she was not in for a happily ever after of any kind, and that frightened her.

Nick was overjoyed at how excited Katriona was with her new dress. It was the first time he'd ever done something like that for a lass and he liked the way it felt. It not only made Katriona happy, but he himself was walking on a cloud. She was so beautiful, especially when she smiled. She hadn't done that very often since he'd first met her, and he made a pledge to himself that he'd see that same joyful face he was seeing now, as often as possible. It would become his duty to make the fair Katriona smile.

Nick hated to leave her, but it wouldn't be right for him to help her with the dress. He closed the door behind him and left her to try on her dress in privacy, telling her he'd send one of his sisters to aid her. As he passed by Isla's chamber he knocked on the door. He knew she'd be preparing her room for their visitors.

"Isla? Are ye in there?" Nick called. "Aye." She opened the door, eyeing him speculatively. "What do ye want?"

"Would ye mind helping Katriona? I bought her a new dress and she needs some help trying it on and making sure it fits properly."

"I'm sorry. I dinnae believe I heard ye correctly.

Did ye say ye…"

"Aye. This is nae time to be difficult, Isla.

Katriona really needs ye."

"All right. All right. I'm on me way. I cannae wait to see what ye've picked out for her. Does she like it?" Again, she eyed him skeptically."

"Aye. I believe she loves it. Now go, before she ties herself up in a knot trying to lace the back." He spun on his heel and headed down the stairs. His sisters, while he adored them, were always needling him about one thing or another. He supposed he deserved it most of the time, but this time he'd done something genuinely nice for Katriona. Not because he expected anything in return, but simply because he had grown quite fond of her and he wanted her to be happy. Was there anything wrong with that?

Kat nearly jumped out of her skin at the knock on the door, she'd been so busy daydreaming about Nick and her new dress. "Who's there?"

"'Tis me, Isla. Me brother said ye needed some help."

"Come in," Kat opened the door to allow Isla to enter.

Isla immediately went to the bed where the dress had been laid out. She appeared suitably impressed. "I cannae believe my brother bought this for ye."

Kat wasn't sure what she meant by that. "Isn't it proper for a man to by a dress for a woman?"

"Oh, aye. 'Tis proper. 'Tis unlikely, but proper nonetheless." She ran her hands over the fabric. "'Tis verra pretty. 'Twill be lovely on ye." She held the dress up and beckoned Kat over. "Here, step in and I'll lace up the back once ye've got it on."

Kat did as she was told and then held her breath as Isla did up the laces, cinching them tightly. "I think that's a little tight. I can hardly breathe," Kat gasped.

"Oh. I'm sorry. I'll let them out a bit." When she was done, she stood back and admired her work. "Ye are beautiful, Katriona. 'Tis the perfect color for ye."

"Do ye really think so," Katriona asked.

"Aye. Try on the jewels and here are yer shoes." Isla retrieved the items and handed them to her.

Kat completed the ensemble and stood back for Isla to see.

"'Tis perfection. Nay need to alter it in any way. Ye'll be turning many a head at the celebration." Isla completed a turn around Kat and came to a halt in front of her.

"I'm not interested in turning heads," Kat responded. But if she were to turn any, she only wished to turn Nick's.

Nick was enjoying the feeling he got from presenting Kat with her gifts. She had seemed so surprised at it that he wondered if no one had ever given her gifts before.

She certainly deserved to be treated like a princess. In his eyes she was. He still knew little about her past, but he had serious questions about her version of what had happened before she was sold to Calhoun. Maybe once she trusted him more she'd tell him the truth. He wouldn't hold it against her. She had her reasons and he understood that. After all, he had secrets of his own, which he wasn't willing to share. She'd been through some very rough times and he felt it was his duty to make it better for her.

His brother, Duncan, approached him as he entered the courtyard. "Where is yer bride?" he teased.

"She's busy trying on the gifts that I purchased for her when I went into town."

"Gifts?" Duncan acted as if he couldn't believe Nick would ever do such a thing. "Ye must truly love the lass."

"Nae. We are friends and for the purpose of avoiding marriage to Skye, we are married."

"Still. I dinnae believe I ever remember ye buying a lass anything."

"She is afeared of Bearach Calhoun. She's been through a rough time. I wanted to make her happy, if only for a short while." Nick was tiring of this conversation. He decided to end it. "I dinnae see ye with a lass of yer own, Duncan."

Duncan had no response to what his brother said to him and so as Nick wished, the conversation about love ceased, but he knew it was not over. He really had developed feelings for Kat. He wanted her for his own, but it couldnae be until her marriage to Bearach was nae more. He needed to deal with that and soon.

That night, Isla and Merry brought their things in to her room. The three would share a bed, which luckily was quite big. She enjoyed having them there with her. They laughed and talked until the wee hours. Kat considered herself lucky. In her real world she didn't have any sisters and not many friends, being that she was always away in some remote area collecting artifacts at archeological sites, or from people who'd found things in their attics or on their property. This didn't leave much time for socializing and she realized now how much she'd been missing out on in life.

Isla was a little rough around the edges. She was a beautiful girl, but she was a definite cynic. Merry on the other hand, lived up to her name. She was always smiling and happy. Rarely did Kat ever see her without a smile on her lips and some kind words to say. They were different, but together they were just what Kat needed.

"Our Nick is quite taken with you," Merry was saying.

"No. He couldn't possibly be. We're just friends."

Kat's face warmed at the mention of Nick and she moved closer to the hearth and farther away from the sisters to hide her embarrassment.

"Believe me, he is." Merry looked to her sister for help.

"Aye. He must be. He spends all his free time with ye and he bought ye some beautiful things." Isla sat propped up in bed as did her sister.

Kat thought about this for a moment. What would it be like to have Nick as more than a friend? She had grown quite fond of him. He was always kind to her, he listened to what she had to say as if she were the most fascinating creature on earth and he made her feel things she'd never felt before. Things she'd only dreamed of, but never thought could happen for her. He held her hand when they walked. She had thought that was just out of kindness and to keep her from falling over, which she seemed to have a habit of doing. She liked him a lot and realized that she had perhaps developed even stronger feelings for him. She wanted to be more than just friends, but she really didn't think that was possible. Her main focus at this time was not getting caught by Bearach Calhoun and to get back to her own time. How crazy that in all her years she'd never met a man who made her tingle when he touched her, a man who, when he gazed into her eyes, made her feel like she were the only woman on earth. It wasn't until now, when she inexplicably found herself in the sixteenth century, that she'd possibly met the man of her dreams.

She still hadn't told him the truth about where she was from or for that matter, what had really happened before she was forced to marry Bearach. She simply couldn't. He'd never believe her. He'd probably think she was crazy and then he'd never want to have anything to do with her again.

Kat was nervous about the celebration the next night. She wasn't sure what to expect. There would be many people present whom she hadn't had the pleasure of meeting yet. Nick promised to be right by her side throughout it all. He told her to follow his lead and he'd make sure there were no missteps to cause them problems.

She would have to trust him. She had to this point and he hadn't disappointed her. Trust was something she didn't give lightly anymore, especially after the horrid situation she found herself in upon arrival here in this time. Nick was trustworthy. Nick made her feel special. Nick made her happy. Nick was her pretend husband and she may as well enjoy it while she could.

"Where have ye gone off to, Kat?" Isla was eyeing her quizzically. Apparently she had gone off into her own little world while the two sisters were deep in conversation. She'd almost forgotten they were there until Isla spoke.

"I'm sorry. I guess I'm just tired." Kat walked to the bed and climbed in.

"Ye look more like yer having some romantic dream." The two sisters giggled at her and then obviously felt bad.

"We're sorry fer laughing. Ye just had such a dreamy expression on yer face. We sat here and watched ye fer several minutes before Isla said anything," Merry explained.

"It's okay. I was thinking about how nice it is to be here with you and your family. I don't have any sisters, so I've been enjoying your company." She almost forgot that they all thought her family had been killed by highwaymen. She couldn't afford to slip up and say or do the wrong thing. She thought to change the subject. "Did you believe Nick when he said he went to the land of the faeries? Could it be true it was his home for two whole years?"

"If Nick said it, then it must be true. He'd never lie to us about anything."

Kat thought that was good to know, but she still didn't believe that story at all. There were no such things as faeries. It was all folklore. Of course, she hadn't believed in time-travel either until she found herself experiencing it.

10

Those guests not staying at the castle had been arriving all day and the Mackall clan was sure to ply them with food and drink from the earliest of visitors to those who were just arriving before the celebratory feast was to be served. Nick escorted Kat to her seat at the head table and then sat next to her.

"Ye look more lovely than the sun shining after a long rain. Ye are truly beautiful. I'm happy to call ye wife." Nick leaned in and kissed her cheek, his warm breath brushing her ear as he did so.

"Nick, we're not really married." Kat said, obviously feeling awkward with his attention.

"Now Kat, how are we going to convince our guests that we're husband and wife if ye keep saying things like that?" He smiled lovingly at her and he could see she was thinking about what he'd said. Should he tell her how he truly felt and if he did, would she believe him?

"Of course, my husband," she said.

Nick was enjoying this little ruse and liked the way she'd called him husband. He was more than attracted to Kat. Over the last two weeks, his feelings for her had grown. He truly felt as if she could be his wife and he would be a most happy man for the rest of his days. The only thing standing in his way was Bearach Calhoun. "I feel fairly certain we can have yer marriage to Bearach annulled. It was a clandestine marriage, was it not?" Nick spoke in a soft whisper to keep their conversation private.

"Clandestine? I guess you could call it that. I thought it strange that there was no priest there to perform the ceremony. It was just

Bearach, Earnan and Bearach's men. They tried to force me to exchange consent with Bearach, but I refused. More than a few of my bruises came from those refusals. When they saw that they couldn't convince me to consent, they said it didn't matter if I did so or not. They were all witness to the vow exchange and they would swear to anyone who might question it, that we were indeed married."

"We'll go to the Bishop of Caithness and explain yer situation. He'll see to it that yer marriage is annulled. Then ye'll be free to…"

"Free to what? Free to roam the countryside trying to find my place in this world."

Nick wrinkled his brow at her words. What did she mean "this world?" "Aye. Free to do as ye wish and marry who ye like."

"That's not likely. I have to get back to my home." "I thought yer family had all been killed by the highwaymen. Where would ye go?" Nick was worried she planned to leave.

"Yes. They were." she stammered. "But I still have some relatives back in Edinburgh. I would go to them."

"Well, I'll take ye to them then. If that's what ye truly wish." Nick wasn't happy about this turn of events.

"It is," Kat assured him.

Nick felt deflated. He thought as his feelings for Kat had grown, that she too felt something for him. He was disappointed to find that he was wrong. He could have sworn it by the way she smiled at him and teased him. Maybe there was more to love than that. His friend Richard had been in love and it had seemed so painful at times. Nick was feeling pain now at Kat's wanting to leave Dunaill. He felt like someone had just punched him in the stomach. The air had been taken right out of him.

When had he come to love Katriona? It had happened without him even knowing it and unfortunately, she didn't feel the same. Perhaps this was the reason he had never fallen in love before. Perhaps he'd always known it would be best to avoid the hurt that came along with the loving.

Lettie Mackall stood on her chair with the help of her sons Rory and Duncan. "Can I have yer attention please?" She called out over the crowd seated and awaiting the feast. The room became silent and when it finally was, she spoke again. "I want to welcome ye all to Dunaill. The Clan Mackall is so happy to have ye here as our guests. We are celebrating two things this night. The first being the return of my son, and the Laird of Clan Mackall, Nicholas." She turned in

Nick's direction and held up her cup in salute. "The second is the marriage of my son, Nicholas and the lovely Katriona.

May they live a long and happy life together." Again, she raised her cup. "Let us all raise our cups to toast the happy couple. *A h-uile la sona dhuibh's gun la idir dona dhuibh*! May all your days be happy ones!"

Everyone raised their glasses and drank. Everyone except Domhnall Maguire, who sat with a grim expression plastered across his face. Skye was in attendance as well, with her husband-to-be, Taran. They seemed quite happy and toasted the newly married couple along with everyone else. Domhnall looked expectantly around the room, as though searching for something. Nick watched him and followed the path that Domhnall had taken with his own eyes. He saw nothing out of the ordinary and chalked it up to Maguire's unhappiness that his daughter wouldnae marry a Mackall.

Servants brought trays laden with all sort of delicacies. There were roasts of all kinds, salmon and trout and delicious puddings all decorated beautifully by the kitchen staff. It wasn't often that they had the chance to impress the Mackall Clan and their friends with their abilities, so they had gone all out for this feast.

"Everything is so pretty. I almost hate to eat it." Kat said.

"If ye dinnae, their feelings will be hurt. 'Tis meant to be eaten." And proving his point, he helped himself to some of the roast lamb and the salmon. "May I serve ye, my love?"

Kat wrinkled her nose at him. "Yes, please."

He was sure she was balking at the "my love," but he was having fun saying it, knowing that it would get a reaction from her. He placed the food on her trencher, being careful not to give her too much of any one thing. He hoped he hadn't given her too much, but he'd eat whatever she couldn't finish.

"I don't know what half of this is." Kat appeared overwhelmed at the sight of the food in front of her.

"Try it. If ye dinnae care for it, I'll take it off yer hands." He smiled knowingly and she shook her head. "Remember, we must look for all the world to be in love." He brushed her cheek softly with the back of his hand and to his surprise, she captured his hand and held it to her face as she leaned into him.

"I'm not sure what is acceptable behavior. I've never been married." Her tongue darted out to flick across her lips.

"Dinnae fear, I willnae allow ye to do anything that would cause concern for the others. I promise." Nick's voice was low, only for her ears.

Kat nodded. "So I take it we can touch each other." She moved her free hand to his hair and gently ran her fingers through his soft brown tresses.

"Aye. Holding hands and touching each other as we've just done is fine." The silky softness of her skin drew him closer still.

"What about kissing? Are we allowed to do that?" Kat's gaze fastened on his lips.

Nick felt his kilt move between his legs. "Aye.

Kissing is acceptable."

"Show me." Her eyes were alight with mischief and something that looked a lot like lust, as she raised her lips to his.

Nick leaned down until his lips were mere inches from her own. He cradled her head in his hands, holding her still so she could not escape. It would nae be seemly if the happy bride pulled away from her man. He lightly brushed his lips over hers and a thrill ran through him. She seemed to feel it as well, because she began to tremble in his arms. Unable to stop himself, he went in for a deeper, longer kiss, enjoying the taste of her on his lips and the feel of her silken mouth against his own. He realized that the room had gone somewhat silent and he reluctantly pulled away. Kat for her part looked starved for another kiss, but he could not oblige. The entire room erupted in cheers and laughter, breaking the moment they had just shared. "So ye see," Nick said, trying to regain some semblance of control. "We can kiss just like that any time ye like."

"Oh," she said, glancing down at her plate with reddened cheeks.

He'd made her blush and he felt quite proud of himself. Next time he'd do more than make her blush.

The meal had ended and the guests were enjoying music and dance inside the great hall. Kat had danced nearly every dance with Nick, her feet fairly flying across the floor. She was quite out of breath after a particularly lengthy song and longed for a rest and perhaps a drink.

Nick seemed to read her mind, as he led her to a quiet corner. "I'll be right back," he said as he went off to get her some cider. She watched him walk away and admired his manly build as he crossed the hall. He was truly a fine man. One she wouldn't mind spending more time with. She'd loved their kiss and being wrapped warmly in his arms all night long while they danced had her wondering what it would be like to spend the rest of the night with him.

"Good evening to ye, Katriona," Shona, the innkeeper's daughter, stood at her side.

"Good evening. Are you enjoying yourself, Shona?" Kat glanced around to see if Duncan was anywhere in the vicinity. She knew they had once been close, but she also knew that something had happened to change things and they now hadn't seen each other in a very long time. "Very much. I've heard a rumor going around that ye arenae really married to Nick. Is that true?" Shona eyed her with a questioning look.

"Where did you hear that?" Kat's stomach dropped. No one other than the immediate family knew their marriage was a ruse.

"Oh, I cannae say. Ye ken how rumors are. They come from all directions, especially in a small village such as ours. I would just warn ye to be careful, 'tis all." She placed a gentle hand on Kat's arm.

"Well, thank you. I appreciate the warning." She didn't get the feeling that Shona was trying to upset her, but rather merely letting her know what she had heard. "Have you seen Duncan this evening?"

"Nay. Well, I've seen him, but we havenae spoken." Shona gazed across the room at Duncan who was enjoying a drink with his brother Rory.

"Why? I mean, you were friends once, what happened?" Kat's curiosity was getting the better of her.

"'Tis nothing I care to discuss. I'll just say we had different ideas about what the future would hold." Shona focused her attention back on Kat.

"I'm sorry. Maybe you should try to speak with him.
It couldn't hurt."

"Or it could. Duncan is a good man, but he's made it clear he doesn't need or want an innkeeper's daughter." Shona glanced away and cleared her throat.

Kat was shocked by Shona's admission, but worked to keep her facial expression neutral. "Are you sure? I can't imagine any of the Mackalls feeling that way."

"Aye. 'Tis truly the way of it." Shona glanced Duncan's way again and this time he was looking back at her. A sad smile crossed his lips and Shona quickly looked away.

Kat made a decision right then and there that she was not going to let these two give up on each other. It broke her heart to see the two of them staring at each other from across the great hall, but she could see that Shona had a stubborn streak and she hadn't heard Duncan's side of the story yet.

"I'd better go," Shona said. "It was lovely speaking with ye."

Kat reach out and took Shona's hand. "I hope to see you again soon. I don't have many friends here other than the Mackalls. I'd like it if we could be friends."

Shona smiled brightly at Kat. "Aye. I'd like that as well."

"Good. Then it's settled. We'll be friends." Kat let go of Shona's hand and gave her a hug, which seemed to startle Shona. *Oh, my, I hope I haven't done the wrong thing.* She questioned the appropriateness of what she'd just done, but then thought, *I really don't care if its acceptable behavior or not. If I want to hug someone I will.*

"I'll say good night to ye. I can see me Da searching fer me." Shona waved good-bye and walked away.

Kat glanced around the room in search of Nick. Where could he have gone? She didn't see him anywhere, but the great hall was very crowded, so she was sure he was there somewhere. She missed him and hoped he'd be back soon. She felt lost without him.

A commotion at the door caught her attention. She was shocked to see Bearach Calhoun and his men push their way into the room. He saw her immediately and as he reached her side, he grabbed her by the hair and began dragging her from the great hall. The fiery pain searing her scalp forced a scream from her lips as she nearly blacked out from the pain. Her feet went out from under her and she was being dragged across the stone floor and out the door before she could work up a second scream. All around her were the sounds of scuffling and shouting. She could see nothing but the angry face of Bearach Calhoun as he swore to her he'd make her pay for what she'd done to him.

They were almost at the horses when he threw her to the ground and reached up a hand to slap her, but before he could land the blow, he was yanked away from her by Nick Mackall and his brothers. Her head was spinning and she felt ill. How had he found her and what was he going to do with her now that he had? She didn't wish to think about it. She had been so happy only moments before and now she knew that her happiness was nearing its end.

Lettie Mackall approached at a run and quickly helped Kat up from the ground and away from the fray she'd been in the middle of. "Dinnae fear, lass. We'll nae let him take ye from us."

The sickening sounds of fists meeting flesh along with the groans of those on the receiving end, were causing Kat great dismay. She couldn't see Nick or Bearach, but she knew they were in the midst of the brawl. Looking back towards the castle doors, she could see the rest of Bearach's men as they lay in varying forms of disarray across the steps. The Mackall guests had seen to it that they were in no condition to join the others as they fought. It seemed like forever before the sound of swords being pulled from their sheathes caught everyone's attention.

Kat had never seen Nick angry. It was a terrifying sight. He looked fit to kill Bearach as the two men stood face to face in the center of the group. "Dinnae ye ever touch her again, do ye understand me, Calhoun?"

"She's my wife. I'll touch her any time I like and in any way that I choose. She deserves to be punished. She tried to kill me." Bearach defiantly stared at the Mackalls who had encircled him. It was obvious he didn't stand a chance of getting out alive if he continued fighting, but it seemed he still didn't understand that he wouldn't be leaving with Kat.

Domhnall Maguire approached. "So, yer wife is already married. It would seem ye can marry my daughter after all." A triumphant smile flashed across his face.

Nick briefly glanced away from Bearach to answer Domhnall, whose smug expression irritated Nick. Maguire took a step back on seeing Nick's anger. "Nae. I cannae and I willnae marry yer daughter. Skye has nae desire to marry me and I willnae take her from the one she loves."

"Love." Domhnall spit out the word. "She'll do as I say and I say she'll marry ye."

Kat leaned heavily on Lettie, her beautiful dress ruined. It was torn and filthy from being dragged through the dirt. Her scalp hurt and she feared she might be missing hair. It felt as if half of it had been torn from her scalp.

"Domhnall, did ye tell Calhoun about Kat being here with us?" Lettie's fiery gaze fell on Maguire.

"Aye. I did," he snarled.

"Do ye nae care that this man intends to do harm to Katriona? She is an innocent victim here, sold to this man and forced into a marriage she didnae wish to be a part of."

"That's not true," Bearach barked out. "She tried to kill me." He was shouting now, aware that everyone in the courtyard was listening. "She deserves her punishment and I deserve my husbandly rights."

"Ye mean yer marriage wasnae consummated?" Lettie asked.

"Nay. She fought me tooth and nail, stabbing me before I had a chance. I intend to take care of that situation immediately upon our return to my castle."

"Well, then. If ye havenae consummated yer marriage and Kat didnae agree to the marriage, 'tis no marriage at all," Lettie concluded. The crowd shouted their agreement and drew closer. It became even more evident that Calhoun would not be leaving with his wife. "Calhoun, ye'd best take yer men and get out of here while yer still able. Go back where ye belong and dinnae dare to come anywhere near Katriona again. Do ye understand me?" Nick growled.

Calhoun narrowed his eyes and mounted his horse. He was joined by his men as they limped to their mounts. "This isnae over, Mackall. She deserves to be punished and if I have my way, she will be."

"Ye'd best hope I never see ye again, because ye willnae be as lucky as ye are this time. I will see to it that ye never lift yer hand to Kat again. Now go before I change me mind."

With one last glare aimed at Nick, Calhoun and his men galloped from the courtyard and out of sight.

Skye and Taran pushed their way through the crowd to face her father. "Da, Taran and I have given our consents to each other. We are married whether ye like it or not and we've consummated our marriage, so ye cannae force me to marry Nick."

Domhnall appeared about to faint. His face went pale, he clutched his chest and called to the heavens, "'Tis all yer fault, Mary. Ye left me alone to raise this pig-headed lass and now look what's happened. She disobeys me at every turn. She's married a man behind me back, a man other than the one I chose for her." He fell to his knees and Skye and Taran ran to him.

"Da. Taran is a good man. He will be a good husband to me, ye'll see." Skye appeared desperate as she pleaded with her father Taran grasped Domhnall's elbow and helped him up from the ground.

"I am a man of my word, Mackall. I made an agreement with yer father when Skye was just a babe. Her mother newly departed, I feared what it would be like to raise a daughter and find her a decent man. Yer father was a good man and so I knew ye'd be as well. I am nae one to break an agreement."

"Domhnall, as the wife of the Mackall, I forgive ye any agreement ye may have made with me husband. Skye has made her choice and Nick has as well. Shall we let them live their lives as they see fit?"

Domhnall thought about this for only a moment and then shook his head in reluctant agreement. "Aye. I only want what's best for ye, me love," he said to his daughter.

"I know, Da." Skye kissed her father's cheek. "Taran is what's best for me," she assured him.

"I'll take good care of her, sir." Taran was still holding onto Domhnall in case he were to fall again.

"Do ye promise?" He glanced up at his new son-in-law as if seeing him for the first time.

"Aye. I do, sir." Taran offered Maguire his hand and it was accepted.

"Then we will have a real marriage, one we can celebrate with all our friends and family." He turned to Nick. "I apologize to ye, Nick. I'm sorry to have ruined yer special celebration. When Osgar told me that ye werenae truly married to this lass, well I lost me temper. He told me about Calhoun and I contacted him with the information on where he could find his wife. I apologize to ye as well lass. I hope he hasnae hurt ye too badly."

Kat was unable to speak. She was so terrified that she merely stood there, looking as if she might fall at any moment and clutching Lettie's arm for support.

Nick quickly strode to Kat's side, taking her in his arms and picking her up, he carried her inside. The remaining guests stood milling about the courtyard, the murmur of their voices carrying all the way inside. "Kat, are ye all right, love?"

"I'll be fine. My head hurts where he pulled my hair and he ruined the beautiful dress you bought me." Tears stung her eyes, but she brushed them away.

"I can always buy ye another. 'Tis ye I'm concerned about. I'm so sorry I wasnae quick enough to stop him from dragging ye outside."

"It's not your fault. That man is a horrible, horrible person." The last thing she wanted was for Nick to feel responsible for her situation.

"I should have killed him when I had the chance," he growled.

"No, I should have killed him and then this would never have happened." Kat had never had a mean bone in her body, and despite her words, she doubted she'd have been able to go through with it.

"I'm going to speak with the innkeeper about his wagging tongue and the damage it's caused. He's here somewhere. I saw him earlier." He glanced around at the people gathered in the great hall.

"Nick, please don't. Leave the man be. He probably had no idea this would happen." Kat was still feeling nauseous from the adrenaline rush she experienced courtesy of Laird Calhoun. Her fears had become a reality. He knew where she was now and he'd come in search of her again. She just knew it. "I'm going to have to leave."

"Nay. Ye must stay. I can protect ye. I promise ye that I will. I know that it doesn't seem likely I can based on what's happened here tonight, but I'm prepared for him now." Nick was pleading with her and it was breaking her heart.

"I want to go home, Nick. I can't live in fear of what will happen if he gets me some day when you're *not* here. I'll be safe if I can just get home."

Nick held her close and touched his forehead to hers. "Please stay, Kat. I want ye to stay." There was a sad resignation in his voice, almost as if he already knew her response.

She was touched by his words and if she'd heard them a short while ago, she would have stayed without question, but now her life depended on leaving. Bearach knew where she was and she didn't doubt for a minute he'd continue to stalk her, biding his time until he found her alone. She shivered at the thought. "Let's not talk about it tonight. You have guests to see to and I'm sure I look a mess. If you don't mind, I think I'll go to bed."

"Aye. I imagine this has been a traumatic experience fer ye." Nick, who had continued to hold her in his arms while they talked, now carried her up the stairs to her room. Without putting her down he opened the door and brought her across the room, where he gently laid her on the bed. "I'm sorry, Kat. I wish I had done a better job of protecting ye." He gently kissed her forehead and lovingly caressed her cheek, before turning and walking from the room.

Kat's heart was broken as she watched him leave, knowing he would never be hers.

A short while later, Isla, Merry and Lettie came through the door. They brought a basin of water, soap and a washcloth. They gently helped her from her dress and put a linen shift on her.

"Dinnae worry about the dress, Kat dear. We can fix it. Ye'll see." Lettie brushed her hair, all the while being careful not to hurt her. "Calhoun is a dreadful man. He'd best never darken our door again. I'll run him through me self." She put the brush down and took one more appraising glance at Kat. Ye look as beautiful as ye ever did."

"Aye. Ye do," Isla said. "Here ye go. Climb on into the bed. Merry and I will join ye shortly, won't we Merry?"

"Aye. We will. And if ye dinnae fall asleep before we get back, we've much gossip to share with ye."

Kat smiled reassuringly at them. They were so kind to want to care for her, she wished she could stay and be a part of this family, but it was not meant to be.

11

Nick was angry with himself for his inability to protect Katriona from that bastard Calhoun. He'd only stepped away for a moment and fate had made it impossible for him to get to her without going through Calhoun's armed men first. By the time he'd reached her, the damage had been done. Kat had gone back into her shell and no longer trusted him to be her protector. He had to win her trust back somehow. He only hoped he could keep her from running away. He understood her fear and knew that if he were Kat, he would be skeptical that anyone at Dunaill could protect her. His frustration was such that he wanted to hit the first person he came across.

To that end, Nicholas saddled up Laoch and headed into the village. He'd have something to say to that meddlesome innkeeper. It was because of him that Kat was hurt and he had a need to visit the man and find out why he'd betrayed them. As he rode, Nick cooled off, going from ready to tear the innkeeper's head off to merely wanting to rattle some fear into him. It wasn't a long ride to the village and the cool air was slowly clearing his head. Once he arrived at the inn and dismounted, he handed his horse over to Rabbie, the inn's stable boy. "I won't be long, so there's no need to remove his saddle." The boy nodded and walked away with Laoch following.

Entering the inn, Nick immediately spotted Osgar seated in a back corner of the dining room, gossiping with another villager.

"Ye gossip worse than an old woman, Osgar," Nick spat out as he grabbed Osgar by the shirt collar and hauled him up from his seat.

Osgar began to shake and cry from fear. "I'm sorry, Sir Nick. I didnae mean to cause ye any trouble, especially nae on yer celebration day. I had nae idea that Maguire would search out the lass's husband."

Nick dropped him back into his chair, where the man cowered. "See to it that ye never spread another word of gossip regarding the Mackalls or ye'll have me to answer to and it willnae go as well for ye as it did today." Nick turned and strode from the inn. The stable boy was waiting for him and handed Laoch over with a nod of his head.

Control was something Nick had learned over the years. He didn't always have the luxury of controlling what was happening around him, but he did have control over how he reacted and today Osgar was lucky that by the time he'd reached the inn, he'd cooled off. He had no doubt that Osgar would be keeping his mouth shut from now on. Now to convince Kat that there was good reason for her to stay and to grant him her trust once again.

Kat sat alone by the window of her room gazing out on Mackall lands, saddened by the predicament she now found herself in. Nick was as sweet as could be and it would be easy to love him. In fact, she thought she might already love him, but theirs was a love that could never be. She didn't belong here among these people. This world was dangerous to her as she'd found out on more than one occasion. Nick tried his best to protect her and take care of her, but even he couldn't manage to stop Bearach Calhoun from getting to her. Now she had to find a way out of this mess. She realized that what she needed was that emerald. It had disappeared from her hand while she was in transit from her own time to Nick's time. Where it was now was anyone's guess, but she knew that if she stood any chance at all of going home, she'd need to find it. She needed to get back to the sight of the archeological dig at Sinclair Castle. Once there, she hoped that the emerald would be in the same place she'd found it. There was no way of knowing where it had come from or how it got there. Would it be visible to her in this time period? It had to be. Why else would it have deposited her here at this time in history? The fact that there was a possibility of finding it, cheered Kat immensely, as did the sight of Nicholas Mackall riding like the wind back to the castle.

Seeing Nick brought a smile to her lips and warmth to her heart. He was such a handsome man, but more than that he was a good man. A man to be trusted. He was her trusted highlander, but as much as she put her faith in him, she still had to get out of this time and back to her own. Bearach Calhoun didn't seem at all intimidated by the Mackalls. He'd be back for her, she could feel it in her bones. What would happen then could be nothing but bad. She thought about all those times she'd thought her life in twenty-first century London was boring.

She'd give anything for boring right about now. Although, she had never felt quite as alive as she did in this moment.

Nick was getting closer and she couldn't seem to stop herself from running down the stairs to greet him as he returned. She opened the castle doors just as he entered the courtyard. His eyes met hers and they shared a moment of recognizing the other's heart and knowing what they both wanted. He vaulted down from his horse, handing the reins over to Jed, the stable boy, with barely a look in his direction. His eyes never left hers as he approached the doorway. Kat's heart beat a little faster and the butterflies in her stomach frantically fluttered their wings in an attempt to get out.

Nick strode to the castle entry with eyes only for the lass waiting in the doorway. Katriona was a vision and she took his breath away. Her sea green eyes were pulling him in and he was helpless to stop himself from what he was about to do.

"Katriona." His voice was husky with desire as he swept her up in his arms and kissed her passionately. He felt her soften and then pull him closer as she placed her hands behind his neck and tangled her fingers in his hair. He was surprised that she didn't balk. Had he been thinking, he might have approached this differently.

After her experience with Calhoun, she had not wished for him to get too close. At least not in an intimate way. The kisses they'd shared at the feast had been sweeter than he'd imagined they could be, but he also thought they may have been just for show. And yet, here she was softly returning his kisses and caressing him with her body.

"Ahem," Lettie said as she approached from behind Nick. "This is neither the time nor the place for that." She brushed past them and into the castle.

As much as he hated to admit it, his mother was right and a quick glance behind him proved her point. They had obviously made a spectacle of themselves as everyone within eyeshot was now standing and staring at them. Kat turned an appropriate shade of pink and Nick quickly turned her and led her through the castle doors, but not before he heard some whistling and good natured shouting coming from behind.

Kat was surprised at herself. She'd allowed Nick to kiss her again and she'd kissed him back, not once thinking about that horrible night with Bearach. Nick had been able to scale that wall and take down that barrier. She was also embarrassed. What did she think she was doing? She was in medieval Scotland and who knows what people would now think of her. She was a married woman and she had been seen brazenly kissing one of the Mackall men. She suddenly felt sick to her stomach. Those butterflies were wreaking havoc today. Once inside, Kat bolted for the stairs and her room. She slammed the door behind her and stood in the center of the room with her hands covering her face. Thoughts of that kiss bombarded her with sensations she wished would go away. Her legs were trembling as she made her way to the bed and plunked herself down on it. How was she going to be able to make all of this right?

There was a soft rapping at her door. *Nick!* She ran to the door, opening it to find Lettie with a stern look on her face. Kat immediately dropped her gaze to the floor in embarrassment.

"Katriona, I'm not here to berate ye fer what happened. That was Nick's fault. He knows better than that. Are ye all right?"

Her concern touched Kat's heart. "Yes. I'm fine, but don't blame it all on Nick. I was a willing participant."

"I ken what I saw. Ye obviously have feelings fer each other. My concern is that ye are a married lady until we can get it annulled." Lettie took Kat's hand in her own and led her back to sit by the fire. She sat across from her. "We can petition the Bishop of Caithness. We'll tell him what has occurred and perhaps he'll see things our way and dissolve yer marriage. In fact, I'd be surprised if he didn't."

"Lettie, that would be wonderful, but even if he agrees, I must leave here. I must find my way back home."

Lettie appeared surprised at this, raising an eyebrow and tipping her head in question. "Do ye nae love my Nicholas?"

"I'm not sure how I feel. I definitely have deep feelings for him, but so much has happened to me of late that I'm not sure those feeling are real. Maybe they're a reaction to Nick saving me. I just don't know."

"Where is yer home, lass? I thought yer family were all killed by the highwaymen."

Kat hesitated at that. She could tell Lettie the truth and then they'd probably lock her up somewhere because she was crazy, or she could continue the lie. "Yes. They were killed. I do have other family members in Edinburgh. They aren't aware of what has happened. I should go home and tell them that the others have all been lost."

"Well, of course ye should, lass. First things first; we must get yer marriage to that good for nothing Calhoun annulled. Then we'll see to it that ye get back home. How does that sound to ye?" Lettie smiled warmly at her as she stood and placed a comforting hand on Kat's shoulder.

"Good." Kat thought about this and it seemed the only way she might be able to find the emerald. She hated deceiving these good people, but what choice did she have?

"Will ye join me downstairs?" Lettie headed for the door.

"I'm so embarrassed, Lettie. I don't know if I can face anyone other than you."

"Of course ye can. Ye'll be with me and not a one will dare to do or say anything about what just happened."

"All right then." Kat rose from the chair and joined Lettie. They'd go together and set any wagging tongues to rest.

12

Malcolm was pleased with his progress towards Dunnet Head. He'd been traveling for days and had charmed his way into food and shelter every night. The gentleman he'd waylaid had some coin in his jacket pocket, which he'd not had to use to this point. The horse had been a good one - strong and obedient.

At his last overnight stop, Malcolm had learned that Dunaill was the Mackall stronghold. He wondered if it was the Mackall Clan that Nick belonged to. If so, things were certainly working in his favor. Nick could come in quite handy when he needed to find his way back home after acquiring the sword, but who could this woman be who was there and was supposed to help him? He'd know soon enough. He would be there in another day or two. He hoped she'd make herself known to him, because the sorcerer had given him no help in that department at all. So far he'd had no trouble at all and he wasn't expecting any, even at Dunaill.

As darkness set in, Malcolm arrived at the gates of a rather lackluster and run down castle. The man on the battlements called down to him.

"Good sir, I am in need of some food and a place to stay for the night. Might I hope that the Laird of this wondrous castle could find room for me? My name is Malcolm Granger."

The man disappeared from his sight and he waited patiently for his return, assuming the guard would go announce Malcolm's presence to his laird, but instead the gates opened and he was allowed to enter without question. He dismounted and his horse was taken from him. An obvious servant stood in front of him and beckoned for Malcolm to follow. To Malcolm's surprise, he was led into the great hall of the castle. It wasn't much to look at. His home in San Francisco was much grander than this place. The room was filled with men all seated at tables lining the room. On a raised platform at the far end of the room, sat a slovenly looking man who was stuffing his face in a most uncouth manner. Malcolm assumed this was the laird of the castle. It was obvious there wasn't a lady of the castle based on the dirt and trash covered floors and the man's unwashed appearance.

"Welcome," the man growled in a most unwelcoming way.

"My name is Malcolm Granger, sir. I am passing by on my way to Dunaill and I'm in need of food and a place to sleep for the night."

"Dunaill! What business do ye have there?" The man appeared quite agitated at the mention of Malcolm's destination.

"I was told I could find a woman there who would help me in my endeavors." He had to be careful what he said.

"A woman! Ha! My woman is there and I need help retrieving her. Mayhap ye can help me." He sat up straighter in his chair and let out a large belch. "Me wife has run away and has taken up residence there with Mackall. The one who's been missing nie on two years. I want her back."

"I see. I may be able to help you." Malcolm didn't really care what this man's problems were. His woman was probably smart to run away based on everything Malcolm had seen since his arrival. He'd humor the man, but his main goal was to find the woman who would help him get the sword, not the woman who'd married this sorry fool. *Unless, of course, they are one and the same*, he thought.

"Sit," Laird Calhoun said, beckoning him to a seat beside him. He pounded loudly on the table and a cowering servant appeared. "Get this gentleman some food, you oaf." He cuffed the lad's ear, causing him to curl up to protect himself. "Go on then, or you'll feel me strap."

Malcolm sat in the seat he'd indicated. "I'm afraid I haven't caught your name, kind sir." He was good at this. He gave himself an imaginary pat on the back.

"Laird Bearach Calhoun, but ye may call me Bear." "Bear, it's a pleasure to meet you." The boy arrived with food, which hardly looked appealing, but Malcolm was hungry and if he didn't eat now, he'd be starving by the time he arrived at the Mackall's. "This looks delicious," he lied.

"Me cook is a good one. Enjoy yer food."

Malcolm stuffed the food into his mouth and tried to ignore the fact that it was close to the worst food he'd ever eaten. He drank some of the ale which the servant had presented him in an effort to wash the horrid flavor from his mouth. "What is yer wife's name? I'll need to know it if I'm to locate her."

"Katriona. Katriona Calhoun." Bear spat out. "She'll regret the day she made a fool of me."

Malcolm had a momentary twinge of empathy for Katriona. It likely had not been her choice to marry this man. "Bear, tell me what ye know of the Mackalls."

Bear grumbled a bit to himself before speaking. "Well, they've long been a thorn in me side. The laird died many years ago and his wife took over his position. Her name is Lettie." Calhoun shoveled more food into his mouth and continued speaking as he chewed. Apparently no one had ever told the man it was rude to speak with your mouth full. "I asked her to marry me once and she turned me down without even a moment's consideration, if ye can believe it."

"Foolish woman," Malcolm humored Bear while trying to hide his disgust.

"Aye. She is. She has many sons and two daughters.

Her oldest lad, Nick, has been missing as I've said. He is now back at home and is the new Laird Mackall. He has me wife and he wants to keep her fer himself. I rode there with me men and when I grabbed me wife and tried to drag her back home with me, he and his brothers put a stop to it. He threatened me. I don't take kindly to that." Bear wore an angry scowl as he rubbed his food-covered hands down the front of his surcoat. "I'll bide me time, but he'll pay for that insult."

So, Nick Mackall *was* at Dunaill. Malcolm was joyful at that news. Things were looking up and he had a good feeling about how this was all going to end.

The evening meal was served and the Mackalls all sat in their customary places the family table. Kat had a spot next to Nick and the electrical current running between the two was hard not to notice.

"Duncan, I'd like ye to visit the Bishop of Caithness. We'll see to this annulment for Katriona." Lettie took charge of the conversation.

"Aye, Ma. I'd be happy to go." Duncan glanced down the table at Katriona and smiled warmly. "I can be ready to go in a few days time. Will that do?"

"Aye." Lettie nodded her head in agreement.

"Thank you, but wouldn't it be better for me to go?" Katriona asked. The Mackalls had done so much for her; she hated to cause them more trouble than she already had.

"There's nae need. If the Bishop needs to see ye, he'll come here. Besides, we dinnae wish to tempt fate with Bearach. He's an obstinate man and no doubt he'll be waiting for the opportunity to steal ye away."

Kat didn't have an answer to that. She knew Lettie was right and she was terrified of what would happen if Bearach got his hands on her again.

"Once we have that taken care of, Nick, you will take Katriona back to Edinburgh." Lettie raised her voice loud enough to get Nick's attention as he seemed to be far away with his own thoughts.

Nick's head flew up like a shot. "Why would I do that?"

"Because that's what Kat wishes. She told me so herself. Isn't that right, Kat?" Lettie tipped her head to see Kat.

"Yes. That's right. I must get back home." Kat stared down at the food on her plate. She could feel Nick's tenseness as he spoke. She could feel everything about him. She knew when he was happy, when he was angry, and now she could feel his disappointment that she hadn't spoken to him about this first. The more time she spent with him, the more she could *feel* him. It was hard for her to explain, but it was as if they were connected on some very deep level and she knew him better than she even knew herself. If only she didn't have to leave, but Kat would never feel safe here, not even with Nick to protect her.

"I see," he said, obviously unsure of how to respond to this news.

The conversation came to a grinding halt and everyone ate in an awkward silence. Kat peeked up to see everyone intent on their own trenchers. She snuck a glance in Nick's direction and he wasn't eating. She felt terrible. Nick had a voracious appetite and if he wasn't eating, it was definitely her fault. She couldn't help it though. She had to leave and she couldn't tell him why. He'd think her as crazy as Kat had thought him on hearing his faerie kingdom story. She tentatively reached her hand out and laid it on his arm. When he glanced up, she tipped her head and hoped that he could read the sadness in her eyes. Sadness that said she didn't really want to leave him. Nick placed his hand on top of hers and gave it a squeeze. He smiled a sad smile and then went back to searching his plate, but not eating.

Nick was stunned. Kat was going to leave. He had to find a way to stop her from going because his heart told him he wanted her here by his side, where she could hopefully one day be his wife. He couldn't understand why she was so adamant about leaving. He understood her fear of Bearach Calhoun, but as he'd told her, he would never let any harm come to her at the hands of that evil bastard. There had to be something else. Her story hadn't made a lot of sense, now that he thought about it. If her entire family had died at the hands of highwaymen, why did she nae seem sadder about the loss. She hadnae grieved their deaths that he could recall.

The only thing that rang true was her kidnapping by Earnan Gibb and her obvious sale to Bearach Calhoun. He had to get to the bottom of this, but she was guarding her secret and hadn't slipped even once. Nick was very sure that Kat's family wasnae dead and that her home wasnae in Edinburgh. Her accent was unusual. She had a bit of a Scottish accent, but tinged with an English accent. She may have been born here in Scotland, but based on what he could hear when she spoke, she most likely grew up in England. He'd have to find a way to tactfully get her to tell him the truth.

"Kat, would ye care to walk after the meal?" Not his best idea. It was cold outside after dark. She'd never consent to a walk.

"I'd like that very much," she replied, surprising him.

He nodded his head in acknowledgement and finally took a bite of his food. From the corner of his eye he spied Kat eyeing him. She'd been doing the same thing throughout their meal. He wished more than anything that he could convince her to stay. He'd come to look forward to seeing her smiling face every morning when he came down to break his fast. He loved the way she sought him out during the day, always with some nonsensical reason to see him. She followed him about, asking him questions about every single thing. One would almost believe she was from another time. Nick stopped with his fork halfway to his mouth and turned to see Katriona speaking with his mother. Was it possible? Of course it was; he had first hand knowledge of time-travel. But was *she* from the future? And if she was, no wonder she was in such a hurry to get back there. He'd need time to find the perfect way to find out without letting on that he was suspicious.

Kat bundled herself up in her cape and met Nick at the doors of the castle. He held out his hand for her to take and they walked out into the crystal clear, crisp cold night. The northern lights lit the sky with the most beautiful colors - shades of green, purple, gold and pink. It nearly took her breath away and filled her with wonder as she turned to see them from every direction. She could hardly contain her excitement at seeing them.

They were alone. No others wished to be out and about on a cold night like this. They preferred to stay behind by the fire, where they could keep warm telling stories and drinking whiskey. Despite the frigid temperature, Kat was happy to be by Nick's side. She never felt a moment of worry when he was near and he always seemed to be near. Either she sought him out or the other way around, but the two had become quite inseparable over the last weeks. It would be difficult to leave him, but how could she possibly share her secret with him, let alone stay in this dangerous time.

Feeling a little bold, Katriona put her arm around Nick's trim waist and snuggled up under his arm. She snaked her other hand inside of his cloak to feel the heat of his body and the strength of his physique. She was playing with fire and she knew it, but she didn't care. She had to know what it was like to lay with him, even if it was only once, before she left forever.

"I ken what yer thinking, Kat, but nothing of the kind will be taking place tonight." He smiled down at her upturned face. Her disappointment must have been written in her expression, because Nick hugged her a little closer.

This was completely out of character for Kat. She was a very modest girl by twenty-first century standards. She was always careful when it came to the men in her life, never allowing anything to go further than she thought appropriate. But here with Nick, that all went out the window. She was throwing caution to the wind where he was concerned. "After the annulment?" she asked, a hopeful lilt to her voice.

"Mayhap. 'Tis nae that I dinnae want ye, Kat. I want ye more than I've ever wanted a woman, but I dinnae wish either of us to be heartbroken when ye leave. I think it best that we keep things as they are."

Well, Kat didn't like that answer at all, but she was pretty sure she'd be able to change his mind. After the kiss they'd shared on the steps of the castle, he was all she could think about. No one had ever kissed her like that before and she was afraid no one ever would again once she left. Kat stopped in her tracks and faced him. "All right, if that's what you wish, but it won't be easy for me. You are very pretty, Nick Mackall." She winked and smiled.

"Pretty!" Nick looked suitably insulted. "I'm nae pretty, lass. I am without a doubt the most handsome man ye've ever seen, but I'm by no means pretty!"

Kat laughed. She loved to tease him and he always had a fun response. He was perfect in her eyes.

Everything he did and said only made him more appealing to her. "You are too pretty."

"I'll not hear another word about me being pretty!

Do ye ken?" His mock outrage was making Kat giggle. "How are you going to stop me, you big lug?" Kat turned to face him, hands on her hips and a challenging expression on her face.

"Big lug? What is that?" Nick's expression went from amused to curious and then to mischievous. "I'll show ye how a big lug quiets his woman."

And then her wish came true. He leaned down and placed a soft kiss on her lips, following up with a brush of his thumb. No way he was stopping there. She leaned into him and initiated the next kiss. Her lips parted and his tongue sought hers. The kiss was beyond words. Her brain was addled and her body ceased being able to hold her up. She moaned into his lips and he pulled her tightly to his chest, one hand holding her back and one grabbing her backside.

He broke away, "Ye've been teasing me with that arse for days now. Ye've no idea what ye do to me, Kat." His other hand grabbed her backside and pulled her hips in until she could feel his hardness brushing up against her belly, causing her to squeak in surprise. "Don't be afraid of me, Kat. I'll never harm ye."

"Nick," she pleaded. "I want you so much."

"As I want ye, but we cannae. We must wait fer yer annulment and then…" He was kissing her again and her brain went all foggy. She was having a hard time remembering why it was she needed to leave this man.

13

The windows of Katriona's chamber looked out on the vast expanse of ocean that embraced the rugged coastline of Dunnet Head, giving her a beautiful view all the way to the horizon. The northern lights were still putting on a colorful display which she simply couldn't resist - the color and movement mesmerizing her and creating the perfect background for her thoughts. She sat completely engrossed, thinking about the kisses she'd just shared with Nick. Safely back in her room, Kat debated the merits of staying here at Dunaill or going home to London. First of all, she wasn't even sure she could go back to London, in which case, she'd want nothing more than to spend her days here in Nick Mackall's arms. The way he made her feel was almost too difficult to put into words. When she was with him, nothing else mattered. He became her entire focus, her entire world.

A light tap at the door hardly broke her concentration as she stared out the window. "Come in."

The door opened and she knew right away it was Nick.

Her nose picked up the scent of him - pine and musk filled her senses. She didn't turn to see him, instead waiting for him to come to her, a little nervous about what might happen next.

She felt him behind her as he brushed her hair out of the way and leaned down to slowly kiss her neck. Kat tipped her head and closed her eyes, allowing him all the room he needed to continue lavishing small, soft kisses up and down her neck and onto her shoulder. He moved one hand to her arm and the other tangled in her hair as he held it fisted at the back of her head. His tongue traced a path from shoulder to ear, causing her to shiver in anticipation. He continued kissing and licking and nibbling her ear. The sensations she was feeling were beyond anything she'd ever experienced. Her breath came in short, quick gasps and the feeling emanating from within her core was almost too much to bear. The northern lights exploded in color before her, mimicking the explosion going on inside of her as Nick teased her to the edge of reason. She wanted to turn and kiss him back, but he held her in place, not allowing it. He moved his hands to her breasts, rubbing his calloused fingers across and around her aching nipples.

She wantonly moaned his name, licking her lips in anticipation, wanting him to take her to bed and make her truly his, but he stopped suddenly and completely.

"Good night, my love," he whispered in her ear. "Sweet dreams." And then he was gone.

Nick was quite pleased with himself. Although what he'd just done to Kat had been pure torture for him as well, he wanted her to know what she'd be leaving behind if she decided to go back to her home. She'd have plenty to think about and dream about tonight. He'd seen to that. Unfortunately, he'd be in the same predicament. He'd teased and tormented Kat to the breaking point and now, as his hardened manhood pointed the way back to his own empty chamber, he was kicking himself for not taking her right then and there. It's what they both wanted, but it was better this way. Leaving her in that condition could only benefit him when she realized that she wanted him more than she wanted to leave. Nick had never in his life played this type of game with a woman, but then again none had ever mattered as much to him. None had been this woman. The woman he wanted by his side, in his bed and in his life until he took his last dying breath.

In his chamber he threw himself across his bed and tried to think of anything but Kat. Unfortunately, he couldn't think of a single thing to wipe her glowing face, her sweet scent and soft moans from his mind.

She'd been slowly but surely burrowing her way into his heart and head since the day he'd met her. He couldn't imagine his life without her and if he had his way he wouldn't have to.

How many times had she gotten out of bed and gone to her door, thinking she'd march across the hall to Nick's chamber and climb into bed with him, only to turn around and head back to the warmth of her own. At least a dozen that she could recall. She had barely slept and when she had, it had been fitful and filled with dreams of her handsome highlander making love to her and then leaving her before she reached her climax. The morning's light found her awake and exhausted.

Kat wrapped herself in one of the warm furs from her bed and went to the window. Opening the shutters, she could see the sun was shining brightly, but there were clouds off in the distance, signaling a snowstorm was on the way. A movement at the very edge of Dunnet Head caught her attention and as she looked, she realized it was Nick. What was he doing out so early? He'd apparently been sitting on the rocks and was now returning to the castle. Could he have suffered a sleepless night as well? *It would serve him right*, she thought to herself with a smile. She was even more determined this morning to get what she wanted from him before she left. Duncan would be leaving soon to seek her annulment and then there would be nothing standing in their way. She hurriedly threw on her clothes and headed down to meet Nick at the castle doors.

Thoughts of Katriona were still bombarding him. Even the crashing of the waves against Dunnet Head couldn't wash away the memories of last night's seduction. If he'd had any sense he'd surely have left well enough alone, but instead he had stoked not only Katriona's fire, but his own as well.

The castle door opened as he approached and the object of his torture stood before him seemingly more beautiful than she'd been even the night before. A smile crossed his lips as he saw her standing there welcoming him back home. If only she would always be there waiting for him when he returned. He crossed the threshold and took her in his arms, crushing her mouth with his kiss for only a brief moment and then letting her go. He had surprised her with the kiss and with the suddenness of its end, and Kat grabbed his arm as her legs buckled. Nick wrapped an arm around her waist to steady her and then guided her towards the great hall where they would break their fast with the rest of the Mackalls.

"Good morn to ye," a cheerful Lettie greeted.

"Good morn." Nick went to his mother and kissed her cheek before escorting Kat to her seat and then joining her.

"By the looks of those two, Duncan, ye'd best get to the Bishop as soon as ye can. I dinnae believe they can hold out much longer." Isla smiled impishly at Nick.

"Mind yer tongue, Isla," Lettie reprimanded her. "Sorry, Ma." Looking not at all sorry, Isla shot another triumphant look her brother's way.

"Duncan while yer away, mayhap ye can find a man fer our little sister. That is if ye come across anyone insane enough to take on such a task." Nick knew he'd hit a nerve when Isla threw her napkin to the table and angrily stalked past him and out of the hall.

"Nicholas Mackall, that was uncalled for. Go find yer sister and apologize this instant." Lettie scowled at her eldest son and laird.

Nick hesitated only a moment before rising and going off in search of Isla. For the life of him, he couldn't understand why she enjoyed getting under his skin to the point where he'd say something unsavory right back to her.

Hurrying along the passageway, he spied her just up ahead of him, hell bent on the rear exit of the castle proper.

"Isla," he called to her fleeing back. "Stop, please. I'd like to apologize to ye."

"Dinnae bother, brother. I ken ye know what ye speak of when ye say only an insane man would want me." Isla stopped abruptly, allowing Nick to reach her and turn her to face him.

"I was only teasing back at ye fer what ye said about Kat and me. I didnae mean to hurt yer feelings so. Can ye forgive me?" He gazed into her tear-filled eyes and suddenly felt even worse than he had only moments before. His sister was a true beauty, but difficult. It would take a strong man to tame her and so far none had been up to the task. Isla sent them all cowering on their way with their tails between their legs.

"I'm sorry too, Nick. It's just that ye both look so happy with each other and I'm afraid I'll never find anyone who'll make me feel that way, ye ken."

He pulled Isla into his arms and hugged her tightly. "Sister, ye'll find yer man and when ye do, ye'll both ken. Ye'll see. There is someone out there and he's waiting fer ye, just as ye wait fer him." He was happy to see Isla wipe away her tears and smile up at him.

"Do ye really think so, Nick?" She hopefully asked. "Aye. I do." Nick knew it to be true, but he also knew how hard it was to wait for that someone to appear. "As for Kat, she may nae be staying here much longer.

She wishes to leave and that means she'll be leaving me as well. So, ye see, things are not always as they appear.

"She can't go. You must stop her. You love each other. I've seen it."

"I always thought love was all you needed to make a life with someone, but it seems I've been wrong. If she doesnae wish to stay, I cannae keep her here, I can only hope that somehow she'll change her mind." Nick felt his sister wrap her arms around him in a big hug.

"I love ye, Nicholas Mackall," she said into his chest.

"I love ye, Isla Mackall. I promise I'll nae tease ye again about a husband. Shall we go back and join the others?"

"Aye." Isla smiled up at him and he knew he'd been forgiven.

"Come. I'm verra hungry. Mayhap ye can hear me tummy grumbling from where ye be so near to it." Nick laughed and took Isla by the hand as they headed back to the great hall.

Malcolm Granger drew his horse to a stop far enough away from Dunaill to remain hidden from anyone on its battlements who might spot him. He noted that this castle was much larger than Bear Calhoun's. There were more men patrolling the grounds and they seemed to take their jobs seriously, unlike those at Castle Calhoun.

The gates were open, so he felt confident he'd be allowed to pass through, but what would he do once he got there. He had to give that a moment's thought. As far as Nick Mackall was concerned, he was a stone statue entombed in a rock wall on Campbell land. How was he going to explain his appearance here? And if the woman he sought were truly with Mackall, which was another stumbling block he'd need to find a way around.

Malcolm usually liked to have a good plan in place when it came to his business dealings, but this was different. He was alone and he had no one to bounce ideas off of. He was going to have to do this without the benefit of his men. He wasn't sure what had happened to them. They weren't in the stone tomb with him and when he exited, there was not a soul in sight. He wondered if they'd managed to get back to San Francisco. It didn't matter to him one way or the other. If they'd happened to be here, he knew he could use them to find this woman and to take care of Mackall. That wasn't the case, so he was going to wing it. He'd done that a time or two on his journey and it had worked out well enough to this point. There was no reason it shouldn't work now.

He urged his horse forward and slowly made his way to the castle entrance. No alarm was sounded, but when he reached the gates he was met my several kilted men, barring his entry.

"My name's Malcolm Granger. I'm here to see Nick Mackall."

Nick was in the stable grooming Laoch, when his brother Rory came to tell him there was a man at the gate to see him.

"Who is it?" Nick asked, his curiosity piqued.

"He says his name is Malcolm Granger," Rory replied.

Nick stopped mid-brush stroke and stood perfectly still.

"What's wrong, brother? Ye look as if ye've seen a ghost."

"Are ye sure he said his name was Malcolm Granger?" "Aye." Rory looked concerned.

How on earth did he find me? Nick wondered. "I'll be right there." Nick was shocked. The last time he'd seen Malcolm Granger he had watched in awe as Edna Campbell had turned him into a stone statue and entombed him with the Twin Sword. How was it possible that he had escaped? And why was he here? The first thing he needed to do was arm himself; Granger wasnae to be trusted. He left Laoch's stall and grabbed the sword he'd left leaning on a bale of hay in the aisle of the stable.

In search of Nick, Kat was exiting the castle doors when she saw a very familiar looking man seated atop a dark bay horse at the entry gate to the courtyard. Rory was speaking with him. Kat had a momentary jolt of fear, thinking it might be someone sent by Bearach, but that wasn't where she knew him from. She walked in that direction and as she got closer, it became clearer exactly who this man was.

"Mr. Granger?" Kat questioned. She was sure she appeared as shocked to see him as she actually was.

"Miss Hughes?" Malcolm Granger broke into a huge grin. "What on earth are you doing here?" He dismounted and much to Kat's surprise, he hugged her tightly to him.

She struggled to free herself and she was finally able to pull herself away. "I could ask the same question of you." She couldn't really tell him right here in front of the others. She hoped he'd understand that.

Nick was standing behind her now appearing quite unhappy at what he was seeing. "Malcolm how the hell did ye get... How..." He appeared unable to form his question.

"I'll explain it all to you, if you'll allow me entrance to your castle."

Something very strange was happening here and Kat hoped she'd find out what it was and soon.

"It wouldnae be my first choice, but it seems something is amiss here and I'd like to ken why." Nick glanced her way, the angry scowl still on his face.

Nick directed his men to take Malcolm's horse to the stable and see to it that it got food and a good rub down. "I was nae expecting to see ye ever again. What has happened?" His demeanor was not at all welcoming.

Kat watched the two men. *How does Nick know who Malcolm is? How did Malcolm get here? Could he possibly get her back home?* She had so many thoughts running through her head she almost didn't notice that the two men were headed for the castle doors. She turned and hurried after them.

14

Nick knew he had to be careful here. Malcolm had shown his true colors back in San Francisco when he had taken Nick's friends hostage and demanded to be taken back in time so that he could recover the Twin Sword. He was a dangerous man who had an ulterior motive, of that Nick was certain. Nick's advantage was that Malcolm appeared to be alone and therefore not a threat. Nick knew he could best him in a one on one fight, but here at home, the odds were even more heavily in his favor with all of his brothers and the rest of his men present.

"Explain to me why it is that you've made yer way to my castle and how ye knew I'd be here," Nick demanded.

"I was directed to come here by the one who created the Twin Sword. I did *not*, however, know that you'd be here." Malcolm's eyes seriously seemed as if they might leap right out of his head as he looked around at everything.

Nick noted that Kat entered the castle appearing shocked and surprised about something. "Mr. Granger. How did you get here? Can you help me get back home?"

Nick was astounded. He may have found the answer to all the questions he'd had about Katriona, but it seemed that he now had more. Kat was from the future. She knew Malcolm Granger. But how? "You know this man?"

"I do. I work for him. And how is it that you know him?" Kat was agitated, he could see it in her stance.

"I know him from my time in San Francisco," Nick responded.

"I see. So the faerie kingdom you were transported to was actually the future San Francisco." Kat seemed to be experiencing a mix of feelings. It was obvious she felt betrayed by Nick because he hadn't shared the truth with her, but Nick was feeling betrayed as well. She hadn't told him the whole truth either.

Nick didn't bother answering; instead he turned to Malcolm. "I think you need to tell me everything. Now!"

"Alright. Calm yourself. I've got nothing to hide and you'll hear the whole story as I know it." Malcolm's expression remained stoic as he continued. "I awoke in my stone tomb to the sight of a glowing sword. The Twin Sword. The one I've sought for so many years. I can only assume that the creator of the sword wanted me alive for some reason. He told me that I should come here and find a woman to help me. I would then know what it was he wanted of me and once I accomplish that task, the sword will be mine."

"What is his name?" Nick asked.

"I don't know. He said he couldn't tell me his name.

That the more it was spoken the more his powers were diminished or some such nonsense." Malcolm made himself comfortable in a chair near the fire.

"I'd suggest you find out what his name is and repeat it hundreds of times, because he's never going to give you that sword, no matter what tasks you accomplish for him."

"I believe he feels I'm his equal in many ways." "You know that King James hid that sword because he thought the sword's creator was looking for a puppet he could command."

"I have no doubt I'll be the one who ends up with this sword."

"But at what price?"

"There is no price I wouldn't pay to hold that sword in my hands and to take it back to San Francisco with me."

"Then you're a fool, Granger."

"If I could interrupt, I'm confused. Mr. Granger, is this sword the one you had the team searching for all across Scotland?"

"It is. The reason you couldn't find it was because it had been entombed in rock on Campbell lands. James was afraid of its power. I, however, am not. Katriona, I believe you are the woman I was sent here to find. You are meant to help me. That would likely be why you find yourself here at this time. Did Edna Campbell send you?"

"Edna Campbell? Who's she?"

"So, you didn't travel through the fog to this time?"

"No. I was at an archeological dig searching for more artifacts for your collection and I saw a beautiful emerald lying in the dirt. I don't know how it got there. I'd been carefully digging and had found nothing when it appeared out of nowhere. I picked it up and as soon as it hit the palm of my hand, I found myself dropped in the middle of a dirt road. It was not anywhere near where I had been digging. I was confused and a man approached me and asked if he could help me. I tried to tell him what had happened, but he spoke to me as if I were insane. He said he could help me. I realized pretty quickly what had happened and I trusted the man. He betrayed my trust and sold me to Laird Bearach Calhoun."

"I met Bear yesterday. He wants you back. When I said I was coming here, he asked me to return you to him."

"Ye'll nae be doing that, Granger." Nick drew Kat closer to him.

"I can see yer quite taken with my Miss Hughes, but she's not yours to keep. I'm sure she wants to go back home, isn't that right?" Malcolm directed his question to Kat.

Kat quickly glanced in Nick's direction. She appeared unsure of what to say.

"I can see you don't want to say anything in front of Mackall. I understand."

"No. You don't understand. I do want to go back home, but I think I need that emerald to get there."

Nick had a sinking feeling in the pit of his belly. Kat didn't plan on staying. He already knew she wanted to go home. What difference did it make if home was in this time or another. She didn't want to stay with him. And now that Malcolm had entered the picture, things were only going to get more complicated. He couldn't allow her to leave with Malcolm. He wasn't to be trusted. As for this sorcerer, what could he possibly want with Kat? This was certainly a troubling turn of events. He thought once Edna had encased Malcolm in stone that he and that damn sword would no longer be a threat. Now Malcolm was here, in his home, and he was trying to take Kat away with him. He needed to speak with her before Malcolm convinced her to go with him.

"I need to speak with ye in private, Kat." Nick said. "All right." Kat needed to speak with him too. "Malcolm, if ye'll excuse us. I'll send me brothers in to keep ye company. I'd appreciate it if ye didnae say anything about time-travel."

"I'll try not to," Malcolm chuckled.

"Duncan, Rory!" Nick shouted, hoping they were nearby. Luckily they happened to be entering the castle at that very moment.

"Aye, Nick! Calm yerself, we're here," Rory said. "I need ye to keep our *guest* company while I have a word with Kat."

Kat imagined that the unspoken part of that was *keep an eye on him and don't let him leave*. Nick took her arm and led her from the room. "What is it? What's got you so worried?"

"I dinnae ken how well ye know yer Mr. Granger, but he isnae a good man."

"I've only met him once when he came to Scotland in search of the Twin Sword. He had an army of archeologists working for him and he was determined to find it. I've spoken with him on the phone a time or two, but other than that I don't really know him." She nervously wrung her hands as she spoke. "Now that he knows where it is, what's to stop him from going back to the twenty-first century and securing it?"

"The one who created the sword would never allow it to fall into anyone else's hands. It is merely a tool to achieve his goals."

"What are his goals?"

"I cannae say that I know, but it cannae be fer anything good."

Kat took a moment to think about that. If there was anything she knew about Nick, it was that she could trust him. She couldn't say that about Malcolm Granger. She hardly knew him, but if Nick said he was dangerous, then she believed him. "What are we going to do? Do you have a plan?"

"Not yet. Give me some time. All I know is that we need to stop him and make sure that the sword never falls into his hands or anyone else's."

"Okay. I believe in you Nick. If anyone can do this, I know it's you."

He smiled warmly at her and gently ran his fingers along her jaw-line. "Let's hope your faith in me isnae misguided."

Returning to the great hall, Nick noted that his brothers were very relaxed and seemed to be enjoying their conversation with Malcolm.

"Will ye be joining us for the evening meal, Malcolm," Duncan was asking.

"I'd appreciate a good meal. The last time I ate was last night and I must say that the food at Bear's castle wasnae very good." Malcolm continued using his Scottish accent in the presence of Nick's brothers, drawing a strange querying glance from Nick.

Nick hadn't yet decided what the plan was to be, but he knew he had to keep Malcolm in sight. He couldn't allow him to leave yet. "Duncan, let Ma know we've company. She'll have a room prepared for him."

"Aye, Nick. I look forward to speaking more with ye, Malcolm."

"Of course, Duncan. I've enjoyed sharing my stories with ye."

Rory joined Duncan as he left the hall, leaving Nick and Kat to deal with Malcolm.

"Kat, I'm curious about this emerald that transported you here. I'd love to see it."

"I'm afraid I don't have it. It disappeared once I arrived."

"You have a beautiful castle here, Mackall. You know, I collect artifacts from the medieval era and you have some excellent pieces on display."

"They're not pieces to be collected. They are a part of my home. They always have been and they will continue to be."

"I'll have to search for them when I return home. It would be nice to have them in my collection."

Not if I have anything to say about it, Nick thought.

"Nicholas, do ye need me," Lettie asked as she breezed into the room.

"Aye, Ma. We have a guest. This is Malcolm Granger, an acquaintance of mine. He will be staying with us."

"'Tis a pleasure to meet ye, Malcolm. Welcome to Dunaill. I've got a room prepared fer yer stay. If ye'd like, I'll show ye to it and ye can rest for a while before we eat."

"I'd like that very much, my dear lady. Nick, ye didn't tell me ye had such a lovely mother."

Nick wanted to punch Malcolm. His mother was a smart woman and Nick would speak with her after she showed Malcolm to his room.

"Sir, ye flatter me." Lettie said.

"Ye are a woman who deserves to be flattered." "Stop. Ye'll be making be blush." Lettie indicated that Malcolm should join her as she left the hall.

Once out of earshot, Nick turned to Kat. "Be careful. He is a man who only cares about getting what he wants."

Malcolm worked hard to hide his fascination with the Mackall's authentic medieval castle, all the while conversing with Lettie. Once at the top of the stairs, he asked, "Who do all of these rooms belong to?"

"The family. This is Rory's room, Duncan's and Nick's." She indicated each room as they passed. "Katriona is in this room, and ye'll be just upstairs."

They climbed up to the next level of the castle and Lettie opened the door to the room that would be Malcolm's. "Here we are. I hope ye'll be comfortable here. If ye need anything at all, please dinnae hesitate to ask."

"Thank you, my lady." Malcolm bowed to Lettie. "You have no idea how good it is to be here after some of the places I've found myself in recent weeks."

Lettie smiled, obviously pleased with his comments. "We're happy to have ye. Would ye like to bathe? I can send the boys up with the tub and some water."

"I would. It's been a while and I'm afraid I'm smelling quite ripe." He chuckled and winked at Lettie.

"I've smelled worse," Lettie said. "Someone will be up shortly with yer water." She headed to the door, but before she could exit, Malcolm stopped her.

Knowing that flattery was seemingly getting him everywhere, he couldn't stop himself from asking, "Lettie, are ye married?"

"Widowed for some years now."

"I'm sorry to hear that. A beautiful woman like yerself shouldn't be without a man to cherish her."

"Many have tried, but none could match my dear husband."

"As I would imagine, my lady."

"I'd better go if I'm going to get ye a bath." She hurried from the room and Malcolm chuckled to himself.

He took the opportunity to examine the room he'd be residing in and was impressed with everything he saw. When he got back home, he'd have some redecorating to do in his home. Malcolm had purchased a restaurant in San Francisco that had been designed to look like a medieval castle. He'd remodeled it into a home and he wanted it to be as authentic as possible. Calhoun's castle had been a very poor representation, but Mackall's was more to his liking. He warmed himself by the fire while he waited for his bath and planned his next move.

The evening meal was filled with chatter from everyone but Nick. He didn't seem at all interested in carrying on a conversation with Malcolm, despite Malcolm's efforts to engage him. He was fairly sure that the rest of his family thought him rude, but they didn't know Malcolm like he did and he wasn't about to tell them all the details. No one knew of his life in the future and he preferred to keep it that way.

Kat also was very quiet this evening and Nick appreciated the fact that she was not engaging Malcolm. His dilemma regarding her had grown with Malcolm's arrival. Kat saw him as a way to get back to her home in the twenty-first century and he feared that she would follow him back when he left. She caught him peeking at her and gave him a sweet smile of reassurance. It warmed his heart and set him at ease.

"This has been a delicious meal, Lettie. I don't believe I've had one finer anywhere and I have travelled quite extensively." Malcolm was obviously working on flattering Lettie. He'd have to tell his mother to be careful around Malcolm.

"'Tis kind of ye to say, Malcolm. I'll be sure to tell cook." Lettie smiled warmly in his direction.

"Malcolm, tell us where yer from. I can see yer a Scotsman, but I hear ye speak differently?" Duncan asked as he took a bite out of the roast he'd piled atop his trencher.

"Aye, I can understand yer confusion. I've travelled extensively and I now live quite far away. The land I live in is quite different, but filled with wondrous things." Nick had to admire Malcolm's ability to spin a yarn.

"Such as?" Rory asked. His eyes were as big as saucers and Nick couldn't help chuckling as he watched him. He was concerned about what Malcolm would tell them and he glared a warning in Malcolm's direction.

Malcolm nodded imperceptibly and Nick breathed a sigh of relief. He continued on, telling the family quite the tall tale about the places he'd been and the land where he lived. Everyone, including his sisters, followed his every word.

The meal continued and Nick and Kat didn't participate much in the conversation unless they were spoken to directly, and then their responses were brief. After they were done eating, everyone gathered around the fire to chat some more with Malcolm, who after a short while gracefully bowed out.

"I'm quite tired. I've had a long few days as I've traveled, so if you'll excuse me, I'd like to retire for the evening."

There was a chorus of voices begging him to stay and talk some more.

"I'm afraid I cannot. I'll speak more with you in the morning. Good night." Malcolm headed to the stairs and then up to his room.

Once Nick was sure he was out of earshot, he said, "Be careful of him. He's not the man he appears to be."

"What do ye mean? He's fascinating," Lettie argued. "Yes. He is. I cannae explain why, but just know that he is a dangerous man and behave accordingly. I expect ye will continue to be as generous as ye've been to this point and as welcoming, but keep yerselves on alert. Now, if ye'll excuse me, I'm off to bed as well. Kat, may I walk with ye to yer room?"

Kat put her hand in his and followed him out of the room, calling "Good night," over her shoulder.

15

Kat settled into bed and fell asleep rather quickly, considering the events of the day, but she had been exhausted. At some point, after the castle was quiet, she heard her door open and smiled to herself, thinking it was Nick, come to join her.

"Nick?" she asked, but there was no answer.

As she lay there in total darkness, she could hear him approaching the bed and then before she could speak again, she found a hand covering her mouth.

"Katriona, please don't scream." Malcolm's voice whispered into her ear. "I'd like you to come with me. We're going to find the emerald that brought you here. Mackall doesn't want you to leave, so he'd do nothing but hinder us in our efforts to find it."

He continued to cover her mouth and Kat became concerned at what he was saying. She didn't want to leave in the middle of the night without saying goodbye to everyone. Malcolm slowly removed his hand, but kept it close so that if she screamed he would cover it again.

"Get dressed. We must leave quickly. And be as quiet as possible, we don't want to alert the family."

"But why? I want to say goodbye to Nick; he's right across the hall." She got out of bed and started heading for the door. Malcolm grabbed her and covered her mouth again. "Katriona, you leave me no choice." He pulled his sword from its sheath and held it to her chin. "You will do as I say and do not make a sound. If you do, it will not go well for you. Do you understand?"

Katriona nodded her head, shaking now with fear.

This was her boss, holding her at sword point. Had he lost his mind?

"I *will* have that sword, and the only way I can get it is with your help. I must bring that emerald back to the tomb encasing the sword. Only then will the sorcerer allow me to take the sword, don't you see."

Kat didn't utter a sound. The moonlight shining through the window gave off enough light that she could see where she'd left her clothes. "My clothes are on the chair."

Malcolm walked her over to them and she threw her dress on over her shift. She grabbed her cloak and put on her boots. Malcolm walked her to the door and then opened it quietly, searching the passageway for any stray Mackalls who might happen to be up and about. When he saw no one, he pulled her into the passageway ahead of him and pushed her towards the stairs. She walked slowly, hoping that Nick would come out of his room.

That he'd know she was in danger and he'd rescue her from this crazy man, but he didn't. His door remained closed.

"Move," Malcolm whispered in her ear as he pushed her forward.

Having no choice, Kat picked up her pace and was at the bottom of the stairs in the blink of an eye. They opened the doors, which creaked slightly, but no one seemed to hear. Malcolm led her through the courtyard and into the stable, where Jordy, the stable boy slept in the hay of the first stall.

"Boy, wake up. We need our horses and quickly." Malcolm kicked Jordy in the side to wake him.

"Yes, sir." Jordy sat up and rubbed the sleep from his eyes before rising and heading down the aisle of the stable to find Malcolm's horse and then Kat's. He saddled them up and then before he could say a word, Malcolm hit him over the head, knocking him out.

"Why did you do that?" Kat dropped to her knees at his side.

"Get up. He'd only ring the alarm and we can't have that. Come along." They exited the stable and mounted their horses. As they got to the gate, they had to deal with the posted guard awaiting their approach.

"Where are ye off to at this hour of the night?" he asked.

"We're leaving before the others wake. We didnae wish to disappoint them by not saying goodbye," Malcolm lied.

The guard didn't seem to think that was a good answer, so Malcolm dismounted. He drew his sword before the other man knew what was happening and forced him to open the gate. After it was open, Malcolm used the hilt of his sword to knock him out.

"Let's go. He swung into the saddle and when he noted that Kat wasn't moving, said, "If ye don't come with me now, you'll be forced to ride along with me on my horse. It would be uncomfortable for both of us, so I'd prefer it if you didn't give me any trouble." He flashed his sword in her direction. "Kat, I know that once we've found the emerald, you'll understand why we had to leave without telling anyone. Believe me. I don't want to hurt you or anyone else if I don't have to, but I want that sword and in order to get it I need the emerald. You're the only one who knows where I can find it."

Kat nodded and nudged her horse forward alongside Malcolm.

"Take your horse up to a gallop. We've got to get as far away from here as possible, as quickly as possible." Malcolm watched her carefully and Kat did as he directed and then he followed suit. They flew across the open field beside the castle, away from the ocean and inland. She had no idea at all how to get where they needed to be, but Malcolm seemed to have a natural ability to navigate by the stars and that's what he was doing. Once the sun rose, Kat knew she'd be better able to tell where they were going, but until that time, she was going to have to trust that Malcolm wouldn't get them so lost that no one would find them.

Nick was feeling restless. He couldn't sleep. He'd been tossing and turning for what seemed like the entire night, but had probably only been a few hours. Something was telling him to check on Kat. She was just across the hall, so it would be easy for him to peek his head in the door and see if she was sleeping or if she too were awake. Having Malcolm just upstairs from him had him feeling a strange sense of unease. He rose from his bed and quickly wrapped himself with his plaid and then headed for Kat's room.

He stood in the hallway, feeling guilty for the thoughts that were making their way round and round his brain. He was only there to check on her, he told himself, but he hoped she'd invite him into her bed and into her arms. He was disturbed to find that her door was ajar. He pushed it open further and called her name, "Kat? Are ye awake?"

He waited, but there was no answer. His heart began to race in his chest as he sensed danger. He charged into the room and was met by an empty bed. *Where is she?* Turning on his heel, he quickly made his way up the stairs to Malcolm's room. Again, the door was open and no one was in the bed.

"Damn it." He hurried down the stairs and barged into Duncan's room. "Duncan. I think Malcolm has kidnapped Katriona. They are both gone from their beds. I must stop him."

"I'll come with ye," Duncan said. "We should search the castle grounds first.

"You're right. I'll meet ye downstairs." Nick went back to his room and got himself dressed before running downstairs, where he met Duncan awaiting his arrival. "I'll check the stables. You check the guard house."

Duncan didn't answer, instead opening the castle doors and heading off in the direction of the gate. Nick ran towards the stable, fear had a grip on his heart, but he knew he had to think clearly, so he pushed those thoughts aside and continued on into the stable, where he found Jordy slumped in the middle of the aisle way.

"Jordy? Are ye all right, lad?" He lifted Jordy and propped him up against a nearby stall. Once he saw that Jordy was awake and seemed to be unharmed other than a knot on his head, Nick asked. "What happened?"

"Yer visitors came in and told me to get their horses ready. I did as they asked and that's all I remember until you woke me."

Nick cursed under his breath. "Get my horse ready, Jordy. I'll return for him in a moment."

"Aye, sir."

Nick ran out of the stable and towards the gate just as Duncan came running in his direction. "Malcolm left with Kat. He doesn't know where they went because Malcolm knocked him out."

"Same with Jordy," Nick responded. "I'm going after them, Duncan."

"I'll come with ye. I'll wake Rory and some of the men."

"Meet me here as quickly as you can. Aidan and Lockie can stay here with Ma and keep an eye on things."

"Right." Duncan headed towards the castle with a purposeful stride.

Nick headed back to the stable to get his horse and to tell Jordy they would be in need of Duncan's mount as well. The other men could saddle their own horses, but they needed to get after Malcolm soon, or they'd have trouble catching them.

16

Exhaustion had seeped in. Katriona hadn't slept much the night before, especially since Malcolm had dragged her out of bed in the middle of the night. Now, they'd been astride their horses for hours on end and she could feel herself drifting off to sleep on more than one occasion. She jerked back up, afraid that sleeping equaled falling. Malcolm hadn't said much to her. He seemed completely focused on reaching Sinclair Castle, the place she'd been helping to excavate on the fateful day she'd found that enormous emerald.

Curiously, it had appeared in a spot where she'd been digging for hours and hadn't seen a thing and then there it was lying right on top of the soil, like she was meant to find it. She had learned from Malcolm that the sorcerer who controlled the sword had been put under a spell, which rendered him invisible and trapped in the netherworld. The only way he could escape was if the emerald was reunited with the Twin Sword. That worried her. She couldn't imagine that it was a good thing for this sorcerer to be set free. "Malcolm, aren't you worried that if you bring the emerald to the sorcerer, that he won't let you have the sword as he agreed?"

"We had an agreement. I'm sure he'll abide by it." "But what if he doesn't? You said yourself that the sword would give you all sorts of power to do as you liked in the world. Why wouldn't he want that?"

"Because he's a sorcerer and he doesn't need anymore power. He's already powerful," he replied testily.

"I'm sorry. I just had to ask. It doesn't make sense to me."

"It doesn't have to make sense to you. All you need to concern yourself with is getting back to your own time. Once we get the emerald to our friend, we'll work on returning to the future."

She wasn't so sure that was going to happen either.

This whole thing seemed like an elaborate trick perpetrated by a desperate sorcerer, who no longer wished to be imprisoned. He'd found the perfect fool to carry out his plan. Kat would never have even thought that Malcolm was a fool in the past. She worked for the man. He paid her salary. She never felt she had the right to have any opinion about him, but here she was being dragged across Scotland by the man Nick had warned her not to trust, and she didn't have a very good feeling about where this was all leading. She got the impression she was expendable and that Malcolm could care less about what happened to her as long as he had his sword. "Do you think we can stop soon? I'm exhausted and I'm afraid I'm going to fall off of my horse if I don't sleep."

"There's no time to stop. We'll keep going until it gets dark and then if we can find a safe place, we'll stop to sleep for a few hours."

"Fine. But I'm not responsible if I fall asleep and end up on the ground while we're riding."

"That won't happen. You've managed to stay awake so far. I imagine you can go on for a while longer."

Kat started singing at the top of her lungs. If she had to stay awake, the only thing she could think to do was keep her mind active. Since she didn't really want to communicate any further with Malcolm, she decided singing would do the trick. She sang an old tune she'd learned as a child. The words she sang were hardly correct, but it didn't matter. Kat had to stay awake until nightfall.

Nick, Duncan and his men travelled at breakneck speed through the woods. They'd found evidence that two riders had passed this way. There was no way to determine who those two riders were, but they were fairly certain that they'd been tracking Malcolm and Katriona. Nick was extremely concerned about Kat. He hardly spoke, concentrating on reaching her as soon as possible. If there was one thing he knew, it was that Malcolm would do anything to get his hands on that sword. He'd go after the emerald and Kat was the only one who knew where it was. He had no doubt that once he had the emerald, Kat would no longer be of use to him. He needed to stop him before he could get his hands on that sword and he'd do anything that needed to be done to accomplish that goal.

"They can't be much farther ahead of us," Duncan said. "We're going to need to let the horses rest, Nick."

"Aye." Nick knew his brother was right. Traveling on at the speed they were going would exhaust their mounts to the point where they wouldn't be able to continue tomorrow. "We can stop for the night. Find a place to camp. We need to rest as well. We'll sleep and then be back on our way."

Duncan sent a man off ahead of them as they slowed their mounts. He'd scout out a spot for them to stop where they'd have some shelter from the elements. They'd been lucky that to this point the weather had been in their favor. Tomorrow was another story. A storm could blow in at any moment. Nick worried that Katriona wouldn't be warm enough. He remembered finding her that day in the woods. She'd been nearly frozen. His heart ached at the thought that she might be experiencing any discomfort at the hands of that madman Granger. When he got his hands on him he'd do what he should have done a long time ago.

Duncan's man came back with news that he'd found a spot up ahead for them to stop. They rode until they reached it and each man took care of his trusted steed. The horses had worked hard and deserved to rest even more than the men. They all realized it and took special pains to make sure that their horses were fed and watered and then left to rest.

A fire was started in the middle of the campsite and the weary travelers sat around it, some yawning and others searching their saddle bags for food. They always carried a bag of oats and griddle for just such times.

Once everything was located, Duncan took charge of making the bannocks and while they waited, the griddle was heated on rocks they placed in the fire.

"We'll get to her before any harm comes to her," Duncan reassured his brother.

"I hope so. I'm not doing a verra good job of protecting her. This is twice now I've let someone get to her. The first time I was lucky enough that Bearach wasn't smart enough to spirit her away during a quiet moment when no one else was around, instead of in the middle of the Mackall feast. This time, I can't believe I didn't think to keep watch over Malcolm, even when he was supposedly sleeping. If anything happens to her, Duncan, I'll never forgive myself. She trusted me and I've disappointed her, I'm sure."

"'Tis nae yer fault, Nick. The rest of us were taken in by him and should have been more suspicious. Ye were, but we paid ye no heed. We let him charm us into trusting him. We were all fools." Duncan placed a hand on Nick's shoulder. "Nae matter. She'll be fine. I have nae doubt he willnae hurt her. He needs her to find his gem. We must get to him before he does, because after that I'm nae sure what will happen."

"He needs help to get back to his own time." Nick realized he'd said the wrong thing. "I mean he…"

Duncan interrupted him, "What did ye say? His own time? Explain yerself, brother."

Nick realized he was going to have to tell Duncan the truth. "Duncan, I didnae tell ye the truth about my whereabouts for these past two years. I lied to ye because I knew ye'd think me daft."

"Daft? Did ye nae think we might nae believe yer faerie kingdom story? Tell me everything."

Nick shared his story with Duncan and the other men around the campfire. When he was done, they all sat with mouths agape, staring at him.

"Why do ye look at me like I've two heads? I told ye it would be hard to believe, didnae I? I've told ye the truth, so close yer mouths and stop with yer staring faces."

"I'm sorry, brother. It's just the most unlikely thing I've ever heard, but I believe ye. Ye've seen the future." Duncan shook his head and stared into the fire, eyes wide.

"Aye. What's more, Malcolm Granger and Katriona are *from* the future. They've journeyed back here to our time to retrieve a sword that Malcolm would like to add to his collection of artifacts from this time. Katriona was brought back accidentally, or at least I thought so. The fact that she knows Malcolm and she seems to have been transported here by an item he needs to free the sword, makes me think otherwise."

"I'd have to agree with ye," Duncan said. "But who would pull her back through time?"

"I dinnae ken, but it has something to do with the sword. I doubt we'll know until we catch up with them and squeeze it from Malcolm's lips."

"It will be something I'll be pleased to help ye with," Duncan assured him.

"Thank ye, I know I can always count on ye, Duncan.

Yer me brother and me friend. I'm sorry I wasnae more forth-coming with the story of my whereabouts."

"Ye've told us now and we believe ye, but I, fer one, would like to know of the wonders that will be five hundred years from now."

"Let's go," Malcolm ordered.

Katriona reluctantly rose from the spot she'd tucked herself into by the fire. She was as cold as ice. That was one thing about this time she didn't think she'd ever get used to. She always seemed to be cold. Well, not always. When Nick was near, it was the exact opposite. He warmed her from the inside out.

Malcolm grabbed their horses and gave her a leg up. "Don't move until I say." He mounted his own horse and signaled for Kat to move ahead.

They started off at a walk and shortly thereafter were at a com-fortable canter. If nothing else, it was warming Katriona up. Her fingers were as stiff as a board and she feared frostbite might set in if she didn't get them warm soon. "I need to get my hands warm." She glanced over at Malcolm.

"I can't help you with that. Wrap them in your cloak if you need to."

She hadn't thought of that, but she awkwardly gathered her cloak first around one hand and then the other. Hopefully the horse wouldn't give her any trouble, because if it did, she'd be hard-pressed to get her hands unraveled in time to save herself. It did help though. Maybe if she kept them like that until she'd regained the feeling in her fingers, then she could go back to holding the reins the right way.

"Did that help?" Malcolm asked.

Oddly, he seemed concerned for her comfort. It was the first time since he'd stolen her away with him. "Yes, it did. Thanks for the suggestion."

"Katriona, I'm sorry to have dragged you into this, but it seems that our sorcerer wanted you here for a reason and so you understand I'm sure that I had no choice but to take you with me."

Why was he being apologetic? It hardly seemed necessary, but for some reason he didn't want her to think badly of him. Too late on that one. "Maybe if you'd waited until the morning, Nick would have joined us."

"Nick hates me, and to be honest I'm not too fond of him either."

"Why? What did he ever do to you?"

"I'm not sure I can pinpoint any one thing. I thought to befriend him at first, but he always seemed to rub me the wrong way. He showed me up at every turn."

"Why would you care about that? You're a successful businessman."

"You're right. I am and I don't bow down to anyone.

Nick always seemed better than me." "In what way?"

"The ladies loved him. He's quite charming and seems like the happiest man on earth most of the time. He's not smart enough to know that no one is happy all the time."

"That's not true. Nick is very smart."

"You see, you are the perfect example. I'm rich, successful, and powerful - but the only people drawn to me are those who want to share in my money and power.

Nick never had that problem, but he was always surrounded by people who admired him and wanted to be his friend."

"Still, he was certainly no threat to you." "Only with a sword."

"What?"

"He's one of the best swordsman I've ever seen. Just before we came back in time, he beat me in a competition. He embarrassed me in front of a huge crowd of people, including my own team of men. That was unforgivable."

"So he was just supposed to roll over and play dead."

"Change of subject. Speaking of Nick bores me. Tell me about you, Katriona. Why is a lovely young woman like you still single?"

"How do you know I'm single? You don't know anything about me."

"I know more than you think. I have a complete file on every one of my employees and I make it a point to read them all. Prewitt has an interest in you. Before you deny it, I am completely aware. I have spies everywhere and they tell me many interesting and useful things."

"What could possibly be useful about knowing that Joel and I had dated?"

"To this point it hasn't been useful at all, but you never know when you may need to coerce someone into doing your bidding. I like to keep a few personal notes available to me in case anyone is ever thinking of being uncooperative." Malcolm chuckled.

No wonder Joel always seemed so jumpy at the mention of Malcolm. He was terrified of the man. Did he have any secrets that were being used against him? "How much further do we have to go?"

"There's a village up ahead. I can just see the tops of some cottages. We'll find out when we pass through."

Nick would have noticed both she and Malcolm were missing. She hoped he didn't believe she left of her own accord. She hoped he was following them and would get here soon. The last thing she wanted to do was to give Malcolm that gem.

As they got closer, Kat realized this wasn't a village they were passing through. It was merely a cluster of small cottages.

"Hello?" Malcolm called out as they rode the path between the cottages. No one seemed to be around and just as they were about to pass the last cottage, they saw a man gathering water from a nearby well. "Good day to you, sir. I wonder if you could tell me how much further Castle Sinclair is."

The man nodded and left the water to join them on the road. "Ye'll have another day and a half of riding before ye arrive."

"Where is everyone?" Kat asked.

"Sick. Been ailing nigh on a week now. I'm the only one remained healthy." The man's threadbare clothing and sickly pallor said otherwise.

By now, Malcolm had covered his nose and mouth with his hand. "We must hurry, Katriona."

"I'm so sorry for your troubles, sir. I hope everyone is well quickly." Katriona wished there was something she could do to help, but Malcolm wasn't about to stop for anyone or anything.

"Thank ye, lass. 'Tis my hope as well." The man nodded his head and went back to his water bucket.

Later that day, as the sun was setting, Malcolm begrudgingly stopped to make camp. He wasn't very good at starting a campfire, so Kat did it. She had a flint in the pocket of her cloak and was grateful she did, because as usual, she was freezing. Malcolm gathered firewood and brought it to her. She could see he wasn't one for physical labor, but apparently he knew the fire was a necessity and he wanted to be warm as well. He brought enough to last them through the night.

Not only was Kat cold, but she was also hungry. Starving to be exact. Her stomach was grumbling so loudly, she was sure it would frighten off any wildlife that happened upon their campsite. There was nothing she could do. They had no food. Malcolm hadn't thought of that before he left the castle. She was pretty ornery when she was hungry and it didn't matter to her one iota that Malcolm was her boss. Former boss she corrected mentally. "Very clever of you to bring food along.

You're probably not hungry though," she said sarcastically.

Malcolm cast an angry glance in her direction. Lack of food wasn't leaving him with a bright and sunny disposition. "I'll be back. I'm going to see what I can find."

The thought of running never even entered Kat's mind. She was exhausted, starving and freezing. She didn't want to leave the warmth of the fire she'd created. She made sure it was near a boulder she could sit with her back against. It wasn't the most comfortable place, but it did keep the cool breeze off her back and with the blazing fire in front of her, she was at least comfortably warm. She curled herself up into a tiny ball as she lay on the ground still snug between her boulder and the fire. Sleep came easily and she didn't fight it.

17

After a long day of riding they still hadn't caught up with Malcolm and Kat, but they were approaching a small clearing and some cottages. All was quiet as they approached. The men stopped at the edge of the village and Nick rode through to the last cottage, looking for signs of life. There were none that he could see. He returned to his men. "Something's amiss. The houses are dark and no one's about."

One of his men pointed ahead. "There's smoke rising up from that one cottage."

Nick confirmed what his man was seeing and said, "Wait here. I'll see who lives there and be back." He rode Laoch to the cottage and dismounted. He carefully made his way to the door in the dim light of dusk and knocked. He waited and momentarily the door opened.

"Yes, sir. What can I do for ye?" the man who'd answered the door asked.

"I'm sorry to disturb ye, but I was wondering if ye'd seen a man and a woman pass by this way."

"Aye. I have. They were here early on this morning." "Did ye speak with them?"

"Aye. The man asked how far to Castle Sinclair " "Was the woman all right? Did she look as if she'd been harmed?"

"Nay. She was a lovely lass. Asked after the people and where they be."

"And where would they be?"

"Sick. The man appeared to be in a hurry and could barely wait to get away. The lass said she hoped we would all be well again soon. Verra thoughtful she was."

"Thank ye, sir. Is there anything we can do for ye or the others?" Nick asked, gazing at the darkened cottages.

"Nay. Ye'd be wise to move on." "I'll send help back when I can."

Nick rode back to his men. "The people here are sick, so we'd best not stay. Katriona and Malcolm have passed this way, but earlier today. If we're to catch them, we'd best ride more this evening. We can stop briefly to sleep and then we must be on our way again. I know where they're headed now and I know the best route to take. I believe we can reach it before they do.

Malcolm won't know the quickest route, only the most travelled." He felt better about that. They'd never catch them if they continued on this same route. He led his men off the road and through the fields. They'd take a straight line through field and forest, while Malcolm took a more circuitous route.

As they headed into a wooded area in front of them, Nick thought it would be a good place for them to rest. "We'll stop here for now. Get some rest and something to eat. We'll be off again in a few hours. The moon will be risen and still near to full, so we should be able to find our way in the dark."

They followed the same routine they'd followed the night before, each man taking care of himself and his horse and then returning to lie around the fire to sleep. A few short hours later, they were mounted and ready to go. Nick hoped that by continuing on in the dark of night, they'd be at Castle Sinclair by morning and they could then enlist the help of Aleck Sinclair in their efforts to stop Malcolm and rescue Kat.

Kat and Malcolm were on their way before the sun had risen. It was dark and cold, but Kat was numb to it by now. She didn't complain because she knew she was close to the end of this journey. She only hoped she might be able to get away from Malcolm and seek refuge at the nearby castle. As the sun rose, Kat noted the clouds up ahead of them - they were thick with snow and she had the dreadful feeling they'd be finding themselves in a blizzard before too long. It was deceiving, because the sun was shining on them where they were, but shortly they'd be under those clouds fighting their way through the snow.

Malcolm remained silent. She assumed he was plotting in his head what he was going to do once he had that emerald. Kat hoped she got to it first. She'd put it in her hand and then hopefully, find herself back in her own time. She would have liked to say goodbye to Nick and thank him for trying to help her. She knew he'd feel badly about what had happened, but it wasn't his fault. The only way to prevent what had happened would have been for him to sleep in her room. She would have liked that.

"Why are you smiling like the cat who ate the canary?"

Kat turned her brilliant smile on Malcolm. "Just thinking pleasant thoughts is all."

Malcolm made a sound somewhere between disgust and confusion, but didn't say another word. Kat was happy about that. His interruption had taken her out of her happy place and she wanted back in. She took a deep breath, closed her eyes and envisioned Nick standing in front of her. Those tawny eyes seeing right through her. His face stern, but there was laughter behind those eyes. He couldn't fool her. He tried to appear a tough guy, but he was actually a teddy bear when it came to her. He treated her with the utmost respect, as if she were a fragile flower whose petals would fall if he wasn't careful. The smile was back. Malcolm couldn't take that away from her.

As she expected, it began to snow. Light fluffy flakes at first and then eventually heavy, wet flakes that stuck to their clothes and their horses. The wind had picked up and was blowing right into their faces. She had to put her head down to avoid it and the snow that was blowing out in front of it. They plodded along until Castle Sinclair came into view. Malcolm stopped his horse, his gaze falling on the castle walls in front of them.

"Where was it that you found the gem? Was it inside the castle walls, or outside?"

Kat did her best to acclimate herself. She closed her eyes and pictured the dig site in her mind. They were on the wrong side of the castle in her estimation.

"Well?" Malcolm was impatient for her answer. "It was not inside the castle grounds, but definitely not on this side of the castle. We'd need to ride around to the front corner on the other side. Then from there I'd have to figure out how far away from the walls I found it."

"Damn it. This couldn't be easy, could it? Let's see if we'll be allowed inside. We can make our plans from there."

They urged their horses forward into a trot, but they weren't having it. They were tired and the wind and snow were hitting them square in the face. They put their heads down and trudged on at a slow walk. Malcolm tried again to spur his horse forward, this time using more force. This only caused the horse to buck and then rear, causing Malcolm to fall onto the snow-covered field.

Kat did her best not to laugh, but he certainly got what he deserved. His horse had bolted forward and continued walking. Malcolm would never catch him at this rate. The horse was headed for the castle anyway, so Malcolm would just have to walk. So much for being in a hurry.

"Don't look so smug sitting up there atop your horse, Kat." Malcolm brushed off his clothes and set off in front of her. Kat's horse dutifully followed behind and the smile lighting Kat's face only got brighter.

Laird Sinclair welcomed Nick and his men when they arrived at his gate. Nick explained why they were there and Sinclair agreed to help in any way he could. He was a good man and one who Nick had known his whole life.

They had a friendly relationship and Nick took him at his word when he said he'd assist them.

"Come. Warm yerselves by the fire." Aleck Sinclair motioned for them to follow him. They sat at a table near the fire and Aleck called to his servants to bring food and drink for his guests. "When do ye expect this villain of yers to show himself here?"

"Any time now I would think," Nick responded. "They came by way of the more travelled routes. We came through woods and across streams. The more difficult road, but I knew we'd make it here before them."

"So, this man stole yer woman, is that right?" Aleck asked.

Nick didn't like to lie to his friend, but telling the truth might jeopardize his plan. "Aye. He did. We allowed him into our castle and in the middle of the night he went to her room and took her away."

"Well, I can guarantee ye he willnae leave here with her. Of that ye can be sure." Aleck slapped his hand on the table.

"He's in search of something as well. It's a large emerald that he believes to be on yer land," Nick said.

"I've never seen such a gem. Where exactly is it?" Aleck wore a puzzled expression.

"I'm nae sure. The lass knows. If it's here, she'll find it." Why he was so sure, Nick couldn't say, but he had faith in Kat and believed that she would.

"Ah, so that is why he stole her." Nodding his head in acknowledgment, Aleck gazed earnestly at Nick.

"'Tis."

"If 'tis on me land, then 'tis mine. He has no right to it." Aleck stated.

"I would agree. We must keep him from stealing it away." Nick was thoughtful for a moment. "I'd suggest that before we stop him, we allow him to find the emerald. It would be best if you had it in your possession and it wasn't lying around somewhere for anyone to take. My men and I would hide out of his sight. I'd like to see what he plans to do. Make no mention that we are here."

"I'll go along with whatever it is he tells me, but I'll nae let any harm come to yer lass."

"Thank you, Sinclair. I'll owe ye one." Nick smiled warmly at him.

"Ye'd do the same for me, no need for thanks." He slapped Nick on the back. The food arrived and was placed in front of them along with some warm mulled wine. "This should go a long way to warming ye lads."

"Aleck, on our way here we passed through a small row of crofter's cottages on yer land, I believe. They are suffering from some sickness and need help." Nick gave Aleck the general direction and distance of the cottages.

"I'll send my healer along with some others to aid them. I believe I ken the crofter's ye speak of." Aleck called to one of his men and explained the situation. "Gather Margaret and yer men. Have cook prepare food to take along, enough to feed all of ye and the crofters. Leave as soon as all is ready. Follow Margaret's orders when it comes to those who are ill. I've nae doubt she'll need yer help caring for them." He dismissed his man and joined everyone at the table.

They all dug in, ravenous from their travels. They ate and drank, laughing and exchanging news with Aleck. As they were finishing their meal, one of Aleck's men approached and whispered something into his ear.

"They're here," Aleck announced. "I will welcome them. Fearghus will show ye to a place where ye can wait for word from me."

"Thank ye again for yer help. 'Tis much appreciated."

Nick and his men followed the servant into a room further down the hall, which appeared to be where Aleck conducted castle business.

There was a fire blazing in the hearth and enough seats for them all to sit and wait. They'd know soon enough what Malcolm was up to.

Kat and Malcolm were welcomed into Aleck Sinclair's castle and shown to the great hall where they were greeted by the man himself.

"Welcome to Castle Sinclair. Come warm yerselves. I'll have my servants bring ye some food. I'm sure ye must be hungry."

"We are indeed," Malcolm said.

Kat couldn't be happier to be here. She could feel her fingers and toes coming back to life and her rumbling stomach would soon be filled. This was a treat for her. She'd been working on the archeological dig for this very castle for months. Now she could see with her own eyes what it looked like before it became a mass of crumbled and missing stone. It was a formidable fortress. She noted the curtain wall from the outside, the battlements, the inner and outer bailey and now the great hall of this massive structure. She wondered at its demise. What had caused it to become a pile of historic rubble? Her eyes were filled with wonder as her gaze flicked from one end of the hall to the other.

"Do ye like it, lass?" Aleck Sinclair asked. "I'm sorry. I'm staring at everything. Please forgive me. I've never been in a castle so fine." She fibbed a little on that one. Nick's castle was equally as beautiful. This one fascinated her because she knew what was to become of it and had seen it with her own eyes. This glimpse back in history that she was being given was a gift she would never forget.

"I'm verra happy ye like it." He had a mischievous glint in his eye that Kat couldn't help but notice. "My friend, Nick Mackall's castle is equally as fine I think."

That caught both Malcolm and Kat's attention. "You know Nick Mackall?" Malcolm questioned.

"Aye. I do. Ye've heard of him then?" Again that mischievous glint.

"Yes. We've recently been with he and his family." Malcolm wasn't picking up on the subtle hint Sinclair had directed at Kat.

She couldn't help but think this was no coincidence.

Was Aleck hinting that he knew what was going on? Was Nick here? Had he arrived before them? She prayed he had. He was her only hope of getting out of this mess and possibly back to her own time. Why was it that whenever she thought about leaving, she got an ache in her heart thinking of Nick. She had to go back, didn't she? How could she stay here in this time? Wouldn't it mess things up if she stayed? The people she left behind would miss her. Maybe not. She didn't have any family to speak of. She was an orphan and had grown up in foster care, moving from home to home, never developing a relationship with any of the people she lived with. None of them would even notice she was missing. As for the people she worked with, they were all so focused on their work, they'd hardly notice either. She cast a quick glance in Aleck's direction and he winked at her. She covered the smile on her lips with her hand an coughed.

"Please, come sit." Aleck took Kat's hand and placed it in the crook of his arm, leading her to a seat at the large table by the fire.

"Thank you. This feels good. I've been so cold." "You're safe and warm now, lass." He put extra emphasis on the word safe, but Malcolm didn't seem to notice.

"What brings you out in weather like this?" Aleck directed his question to Malcolm.

"Trying to get Katriona back to Edinburgh. She'd like to reunite with her loved ones."

"Yer not taking the most direct route to that fine city," he observed.

"The weather has not been our friend. It has driven us off course."

"Well, enjoy yer meal and feel free to roam the castle as ye like. I've some things to attend to. I'll be back later to see how ye fare."

"Thank you," Kat said. "Your hospitality is most welcome."

When Aleck and the servants had left the hall, Kat filled her belly. All of her senses were being filled with warmth and good food. The sights, sounds, smells and feel of this place were just right in her mind. It was what she needed to help her to continue on with Malcolm and his crazy scheme. From the looks of it though, Aleck had some idea of what was going on and she felt secure that he wouldn't allow any harm to come to her.

She was just sitting back and relaxing by the fire when Malcolm handed her her cloak. "Come on. Let's see if we can find it while it's still light outside."

"But it's so cold out there." She hoped to delay him until it was too dark to search and then he'd be forced to wait until tomorrow. With any luck Nick would be here by then, if he wasn't here already.

"You've had plenty of time to get warm. Come on.

Now." Malcolm dragged her up out of the chair and threw her cloak over her shoulders. As they exited the hall, they came upon three of Aleck's men. "We're going outside for a short walk." He brushed passed them, again dragging Katriona in his wake.

Once outside they headed for the gate and Malcolm practically pushed Kat out in front of him. "Lead the way," he ordered.

Kat deliberately dragged her feet, slowing to pretend interest in everything. "I'm just trying to get my bearings."

Malcolm was obviously becoming impatient with her. "Hurry up. You should have an idea of at least the area where you found it."

"I have to measure the distance from the corner of the curtain wall out." She set herself at the base of the curtain wall and took large paces in a diagonal direction, counting out loud as she went. Malcolm followed on her heels. As they came to the spot where Kat was sure she'd found the emerald, she scanned the immediate area in search of anything green that might catch her eye. Not an easy task with the ground covered in snow. "This is the spot, but I don't see anything. It may be covered by the snow."

Malcolm immediately dropped to his knees, intent on finding it. "Help me. Between the two of us, we should be able to clear this small area of snow quickly."

Kat didn't want to kneel in the snow. She'd just gotten warmed up and now Malcolm had decided it would be a good idea to add wet to the cold. Of course, Malcolm wasn't having any hesitation on Kat's part. He grabbed her arm and yanked her down into the snow alongside him. "Dig," he ordered.

Doing as she was told, Kat plunged her hands into the icy cold snow, hoping that the faster they got the snow cleared, the faster she'd be back inside the castle and warm once again. They continued like this until she thought the pain in her fingers couldn't possibly get any worse and then she saw it. The green gem that had transported her to this time period sat in a small tuft of grass that had been covered by the snow. She reached out her hand to grab it, hoping that once it hit her palm the same magic that had brought her here would bring her home. Unfortunately, Malcolm spied it at the exact same moment and he was faster than her. He grabbed it away a split second before she could grasp it. He held it up towards the sky, which was still white with snow. The green of the gem sparkled nonetheless. It didn't seem to need sunshine to accomplish this feat. It was a self-made sparkle, coming from deep within the gem itself.

"Magic," Malcolm muttered as he fisted the gem and gazed up to find Nick and his men ready and waiting for him. They weren't alone. Sinclair's men were also present as was the laird himself.

"I believe that gem belongs to me," Aleck stated. "I'm afraid not. It's coming with me, as is Katriona." He grabbed her by the arm and pulled his sword. "Don't try to stop me, or our lovely lass here will meet an unfortunate end." Malcolm pulled Kat closer to him and she shivered in fear. Nick's face was her focus. If she kept her eyes on him, everything would be all right. He wouldn't allow any harm to come to her.

There were so many of them and only one Malcolm, but he had the advantage. He had the gem and he had her. He slowly began to back away from them, but the men fanned out and encircled him.

"Ye won't be leaving here with the gem or the lass." Nick had his hand on the hilt of his sword. "Ye'd be wise to give up now, while ye still can, Malcolm."

"I'll kill her. If you don't believe me, just test me." He dragged Kat back and the men parted to let him through.

Kat was on the verge of panic. She couldn't see Nick now. She flicked her eyes back and forth, but he wasn't there. Where was he? Where had he gone? She needed him.

"Don't even think about it, Mackall!" Malcolm shouted and spun. Nick had made his way behind them and from the looks of it was planning to ambush Malcolm. He stopped dead in his tracks as Malcolm's sword now lay against Kat's throat. "I'll need two horses. Now!"

Aleck nodded to two of his men who dismounted and handed the reins to Malcolm.

"Back away," Malcolm ordered. Nick gazed at her with a softness to his eyes and a sorrowful expression, but he then stared daggers at Malcolm. Kat was shaking. Were they really going to let him leave with her? What choice did they have? It was obvious that Malcolm was a desperate man and as such would have no problem hurting her.

"Malcolm," Nick's calm but menacing voice was clear. "If you so much as harm a hair on her head, you're a dead man."

"If you stay away from us and allow me to get back to the sword, you won't have a thing to worry about." Malcolm shoved Kat towards the horses. "Get up there." He held his sword to her back as she mounted and then he quickly did the same. He slapped the rump of her horse and sent it flying as he spurred his own horse to do the same.

18

Stalking angrily back towards the castle, Nick cursed Malcolm Granger and vowed to make him pay for using Katriona as a shield. "Duncan get the horses saddled and ready to go." Nick barked out orders to his men and then turned to Aleck. "Thank ye much fer yer help.

Unfortunately, Malcolm got the better of us."

"I'm coming with ye, Nick." Aleck motioned to his men to get their horses. "We'll meet here at the gate."

"Aye." Nick hurried towards the stables to retrieve Laoch. His brothers Duncan and Rory, met him as he approached.

"Dinnae fear, Nick, we'll get her back," Duncan assured him.

"Aye, we will." Rory added.

Nick nodded his agreement with his brothers. "Granger will pay dearly for what he's done. We know where they're headed and if we trail them at a safe distance and bide our time, we'll overtake them. We must proceed cautiously so no harm comes to Kat." He sounded confident, but he was extremely worried. What if they didn't get to Malcolm before he got the sword? The man was consumed by the need for power and the sword would give him all he wanted. "I don't believe it's his plan to harm her, but that could all change should he feel at all threatened by our approach." If anything happened to Kat he'd never forgive himself.

Thoughts of escape were running around in Kat's brain, but none of the ideas she'd had seemed as if they'd work. Malcolm was keeping close watch over her. He seemed to know she was waiting for an opportune moment to get away from him and because of it, he was ponying her alongside his steed, leaving her no control over her own horse.

"Once I have the sword in my possession, I should have no problem returning to my own time. You're welcome to join me if you behave yourself."

Malcolm's smug demeanor was wearing on her, but Kat didn't respond. She didn't want to go anywhere with Malcolm, even back to her own time. Malcolm had put his sword away and Kat no longer feared he was planning to use it on her. She had no doubt Nick would be following them and was probably not too far behind. That thought gave her solace - he wouldn't let any harm come to her.

The endless riding was starting to get to her. "Can we stop, please?" Kat begged.

"No. We haven't put enough distance between us and Mackall. We won't be stopping until way after dark, so there's no point in complaining." Malcolm's menacing gaze met hers.

He was trying to shut her up, but it wasn't going to work. "What makes you so sure he's following us?"

"It's obvious the man is in love with you. You do know that, don't you?" He snickered and rolled his eyes heavenward.

Kat didn't respond. She had no doubt he'd come for her, but was it because he loved her or was he simply being a chivalrous highlander who'd do the same for any woman in need? He may have feelings for her, but she doubted it was love. He had been kind, caring and very protective of her, but did that necessarily equal love? Kat knew how she felt about Nick and when she thought about him, she felt as light as air. She tuned Malcolm out and daydreamed about her tawny-eyed highlander and what it would be like to be loved by such a man.

Thinking about Nick took her mind off of her predicament and made the time pass more easily. After a few more hours of riding, it appeared that Malcolm was ready to stop. Darkness would be falling soon and as they came to a halt in a wooded area that opened out on a clearing, Malcolm tensed in his saddle, causing Kat to follow his gaze where she saw a group of mounted men heading their way. She was one hundred percent sure it wasn't Nick. They were coming from the wrong direction and as they got closer, her heart nearly jumped into her throat. It was Bearach Calhoun and his men. They'd seen her and Malcolm and were now headed straight for them.

"I think I'm going to be sick," Kat announced as she clutched her belly.

"It seems your husband has found you." Malcolm chuckled as he waited for Calhoun to come to a stop in front of them.

"Sir, I see ye've found me wife. I thank ye. Yer a man of yer word." Calhoun signaled to his men to grab Kat's horse and Malcolm made no move to stop them.

"You aren't going to let them take me, are you?" Kat asked in disbelief.

"You're really of no further use to me. As a matter of fact, it might get Mackall off of my tail long enough for me to get my sword back and then head home."

"If Nick Mackall's after ye, it'd be best ye return with me to me castle. We can defend against him there."

Malcolm appeared to be weighing his options. "I think I'll take you up on that offer. I really can't travel much farther tonight, but I'll leave before sunrise tomorrow. I don't wish to wear out my welcome."

"Good. Let's get back there then. We'll need time to prepare for Mackall's arrival. He won't get away with stealing my woman, and after we've finished with them," Bearach directed his next comment to Kat, "I'll see to it that ye pay dearly for what ye've done."

Kat's heart sank. She was doomed and even if Nick did come for her, would he be too late or would he end up dead because he'd dared to help her?

Nick and Aleck had stopped within earshot of Malcolm and Calhoun. Their men waited for them further back on the road, so as not to be seen.

"Calhoun!" Nick spat the name from his mouth as if it had a horrible taste. "We've got to get her back before he harms her again."

"Again? What do you mean?" Aleck appeared confused. "He's her husband," Nick answered.

"Her husband?" Aleck's face went from confused to shocked.

"Aye. She was forced to marry the man and suffered greatly by his hand." He continued on, giving Aleck the condensed version of her story. "She's been running from him ever since. I'm afraid of what he'll do if he has even a moment alone with her."

"I see. Well we cannae allow that to happen then. We must overtake them before they are able to enter the castle walls."

The two men listened closely for a few moments longer and then headed back to their men.

"Duncan, Rory, follow them as closely as ye can without being noticed. If Calhoun lays a hand on Kat, signal me so I can intervene. In the meantime, we'll ride further back and when the time is right we'll strike, but it will have to be soon."

"Aye, Nick. We'll take care of it."

Nick was about ready to jump out of his skin, but he knew that it might be more harmful than good for him to act rashly in this situation. He needed to maintain a cool head if he were to be effective. He could see Aleck eyeing him with concern. "Don't worry. I'll nae do something we'll regret," he assured him, but added, "Calhoun will rue the day he forced Kat to be his wife."

"I'll be happy to help ye with that. What of that Malcolm fella?"

"Granger is after the Twin Sword. He wants the power he can achieve by owning it, but the sorcerer who created it also wants it and Malcolm thinks he can outsmart him and win in the end."

"He may nae even get there."

"It would be good if he didnae. I dinnae care to think what havoc he'd bring down upon all our heads if the sorcerer were able to finally wield the sword."

"How is it that you ken this man Granger?"

"We met in a time and place you would be unfamiliar with. He was even then thinking of nothing but the Twin Sword. Now that it's within his grasp, he will be even more dangerous than I ever imagined he could be." Aleck was eyeing him questioningly. Perhaps he'd said too much.

At the sounds of a horse galloping toward them, their heads shot up.

"Nick, something's happening up ahead at the river." Duncan's horse came to a halt by Nick and Aleck. "Calhoun's men were trying to cross when their horses all, every last one, spooked and began bucking and rearing. Some of the men were thrown into the fast moving water and others landed on dry ground. If there ever was a time to attack, now would be that time."

"Let's go then." He signaled back to the men and they all took off at a gallop. As they rounded a bend in the road they saw complete chaos as Bearach and his men tried to regain control of their mounts. Nick scanned the area for Kat and spied her as she hid behind a nearby tree. Granger had just been thrown from his horse and was struggling to stand. Bearach was the only one who didn't appear to have been hurt.

Nick, Aleck and their men raced into the middle of the commotion, swinging their swords and taking on any man brave enough to challenge them. Nick plowed through those who stood between him and Bearach Calhoun. Jumping from his horse, Nick stood to his full height, towering over Calhoun.

Bearach for his part was not about to let Nick take Kat away from him. His head swiveled back and forth as he searched for her. Nick's sword arced through the air right at Bearach's head, but Bearach saw it at the last moment and was able to drop to the ground and roll out of the way. He rose and began thrashing his sword in Nick's direction. Nick stood his ground and waited for Calhoun to come to him. He used all the skill he had in that moment, never once allowing anything to change his focus from the fight at hand. At the rate he was going, Calhoun would be worn out before he even got close enough to Nick to strike and by then, Nick would have the upper hand.

Aleck was busy with Granger, who had regained his feet and was now fighting for all he was worth. He was, however, no match for Aleck, who was easily able to disarm him. Malcolm was furious as he pulled a dagger from his belt and dove headlong toward Aleck, who was waiting for him and cleanly ran him through with his sword. A surprised expression crossed Malcolm's face as he stood momentarily staring at Aleck before falling dead to the ground.

The other men were taking on what was left of Bearach Calhoun's men, those who hadn't been washed down river and those who weren't lying unconscious on the ground. The horses were long gone, having charged away as soon as they were free of their riders.

As for Nick and Bearach, they were engaged in a game of cat and mouse. Nick was obviously the cat and Calhoun the mouse who kept backing further and further away while Nick followed his every move. As they reached a nearby tree, Nick had a sickening feeling in the pit of his belly as Calhoun reached around behind it and dragged a struggling Kat out, holding her in front of him for protection. By now, Aleck and the rest of their men had surrounded him. There was no way he would get out of this alive, but the question was, how to get Kat out of his grasp before he took her with him once again.

"Drop yer weapons," Bearach called out. "If ye dinnae, I'll have to slice this troublesome lassie's throat. Do ye hear me?" He gave Kat a good shake to make his point clear.

"Aye. We hear ye." Nick dropped his sword. He couldn't allow any further harm to come to Kat. He'd find a way to save her yet, but at this moment in time, anything he did would put her life in jeopardy. "Put down yer swords men."

The clattering of swords hitting the ground brought a satisfied smirk to Bearach Calhoun's face, but it would be the last time he'd ever smile again.

What happened next wasn't clear. Katriona was clearly entangled in Bearach's arms one moment and then his grip loosened and she felt him slide down behind her, his hand trailing a path from her neck down to her ankle.

His sword leaving his grip, landed with a thud on the ground beside him. When she looked, his lifeless eyes stared up at her and Nick was there hauling her into his arms and kissing her head.

Kat couldn't stop shaking, the adrenaline rushing through her veins barely kept her rooted in place. She wanted to run so badly, but she knew the danger was finally over, so there was no need. She breathed deeply, the familiar scent of Nick Mackall calming her as she buried her nose in his chest.

"Thank ye, Duncan," Nick said. "I didnae see ye back there. Ye saved Kat's life."

"I ken ye'd do the same fer me, brother.

"Are ye all right, Kat?" He held her away from him just long enough to make sure she wasn't injured and pulled her back into his arms. She was shaking and visibly in shock. After a few moments she seemed to regain control, pushing away from him and rushing to Malcolm Granger's dead body where it lay on the ground.

"Where's the emerald," she cried while frantically searching Malcolm's hand and then the ground.

Nick spied it in the snow. "'Tis there." He pointed to the spot on the ground where it had fallen out of Malcolm's hand. Kat dove for it, but before she could get to it, the gem melted away into the snow and disappeared. She frantically dug around in the snow, tears trailing down her cheeks.

"It's gone. Oh, no! It's gone."

Nick knelt beside her and gently guided her into his arms. She buried her head in his chest and cried. He understood she was grieving the fact that she'd lost her way home. He'd hoped she'd be happy to stay here with him, but seeing her so aggrieved, broke his heart. "Don't worry, lass. We'll find a way to get you back home. I promise." She wrapped her arms around his waist and he walked with her back towards the castle.

Aleck wrapped an arm about them both and Duncan walked along on the opposite side. A few of the men were tasked with disposing of the bodies, but for now they left them where they lay, the white snow now covered with red.

19

Nick cradled Kat in his arms. Having her there was all he'd thought about since he'd found her missing and now that she was back where he felt she belonged, he was going to do his best to make her happy. She'd stay. She had no choice now, but he wanted her to feel at home with him and not be longing to return to the future. He thought about his own time away, when he'd been in the twenty-first century. He'd adapted and he'd been happy. If he'd had to stay, he would have. He'd made friends and he'd made a life for himself while there. He knew Kat could do the same with him. He just needed to let her know what she had come to mean to him.

"You are welcome to stay as long as you like," Aleck told them. "If the gem shows up again, ye'll be the first to know, lass. I'll make sure it gets to ye."

Kat gazed up at him through tear-filled eyes. "Thank you. It's not really mine though."

"I know that, but I believe that while it doesn't belong to ye, it belongs with ye." He gently ran a hand over her hair. "Rest for now, lass. Our Nick will take good care of ye. Ye've nothing to fear now."

Nick gave Aleck a grateful look as Kat laid her head back against his chest, giving him a warm feeling throughout his body. His Katriona, his love. He had barely admitted it to himself, but he knew he must tell her, however, he'd wait until they were alone and the time was right. Saying so now, in front of all those gathered in the great hall, was not what she'd want. He knew that. She'd want romance and wooing and he'd give her all of that and more.

Aleck had accommodations for all of them. The men would sleep in the great hall, which served double duty as a feasting room, a gathering room and when needed sleeping quarters. Duncan was given a room, as was Nick. Aleck hadn't been sure what the sleeping arrangements should be, so he gave Kat her own room and would leave it up to them how the night would go.

"I have no problem if ye wish to share yer bed. If I had a warm and willing lass, I'm sure I would." He smiled warmly at Nick, who sat with Kat nestled in his arms. Thankfully, she was now asleep and hadn't heard their conversation. He wasn't sure what she'd think of that.

"I dinnae wish to let her out of my sight. Every time I do, something bad happens. I'll sleep better if she's near me."

"I cannae say that I blame ye, Nick. I believe she'll be happy with that arrangement from the looks of things."

"We'll bid ye good night then." Nick rose with Kat in his arms and carried her to the chamber they'd been assigned, laying her on the bed and covering her with the fur skins that lay atop the bed. She sighed sweetly, causing Nick's body to react of its own accord. He had to get a grip on himself. He'd sleep on the floor. He'd be close enough that if she needed him, he could be there in an instant, but he wouldn't lay with her without her knowledge. He walked away from her and found a place on the floor to make his bed, but Kat had other plans for him.

"Where are you going?" Kat sat up in the bed, sleepy eyes searching for Nick.

"I won't be far, love. Just here on the floor." Nick moved closer so she could see him in the candlelight.

"Don't sleep on the floor. You'll be uncomfortable.

There's plenty of room for you here next to me."

"I don't wish to compromise your reputation, lass." "It's already compromised. You're in the room with me silly."

"Silly. Are ye calling *me* silly?" Nick gave her a fierce look, but obviously she wasn't taken in by it.

Kat giggled and patted the bed. "Please. I want you to sleep here."

"Well, if ye insist. How can I argue with ye when ye smile at me like that." Nick sat down next to her and gently stroked her cheek. Tucking a stray hair behind her ear, he was enthralled by her. Unable to break his gaze, he said, "Ye ken yer a beauty. I dinnae believe I've ever seen a lass as fair as ye are."

Kat reached out to touch his face and to run a finger across his lips. Nick held his breath. What was she doing? Didn't she ken she was causing him to lose his self-control? Damn it. He was going to kiss her. How could he not? He bent his head down and leaned in closer. Her lips parted and he captured them, kissing her with a mixture of passion, relief and possession.

She was his, but more importantly he was completely and utterly hers. They reluctantly broke the kiss and Kat pulled him down onto the bed to lie beside her. She placed her head on his shoulder and her sweet breath caressed his neck. How was he ever going to get through this night? One moment at a time.

At some point in the middle of the night, Kat wrapped herself around Nick, her leg rubbing against his hardened manhood. He groaned out loud and she purred like a kitten. Her hand moved down his chest to rest on his belly. He was trapped beneath her, a prisoner of her seductive wiles. What was he to do? He was a man, not a saint. Instinct kicked in and he rolled on top of her only to find her smiling face and wide eyes staring up at him.

"Hi," she whispered.

"Hi," he answered, echoing her modern day language.

The world stood still as they each let their eyes roam over the other. Nick gently brushed his lips across hers and her tongue darted out to meet him. She wasn't playing fair. He wanted her, but he wanted to take his time. He wanted their first time together to be special, something to remember, although no matter he couldn't imagine he'd ever forget this moment.

"Are ye sure, Kat?" "I am."

Sweeter words were never spoken. He kissed her again, this time wanting to meld with her. To become one with this beautiful woman who'd somehow managed to make him love her without even trying. He kissed her long and hard and she matched him with fervent ardor.

"Nick, I want you so much. I can't wait." She reached down and wrapped her hand around his swollen shaft, directing it towards her warm, moist folds.

His pleasure was beyond measure. "Kat, let's take our time. I want you to enjoy this as much as me."

"I will. This isn't the only time we're going to do this, is it?" She giggled with a twinkle of knowing in her eyes.

"No, of course not." Nick kissed her neck and nibbled on her earlobe.

Kat guided him towards her center once again and this time he didn't resist. Entering her warmth he thought nothing had ever felt better. He didn't want it to end. Kat writhed in pleasure beneath him, only heightening his own enjoyment. The silky, soft feeling of her womanhood caressed the hardness of his cock. He savored every moment as the feeling built and built to an almost unbearable crescendo. Kat's enjoyment was evident, pleasing him more than he could have imagined. They soared ever higher and finally crested the peak together, Kat calling out his name and Nick roaring his release.

They held onto each other until and long after they both fell into a deep and wonderful sleep.

Kat hadn't slept this well since her arrival in sixteenth-century Scotland. Nick gave her a sense of security she'd never had in her life. People came and went in Kat's life almost from the very beginning. She'd come to expect it and so this feeling was foreign to her, but very, very nice. She snuggled in a little closer and Nick rolled toward her to pull her in even tighter. She placed her nose in the hollow spot just below his Adam's apple and breathed in deeply the scent of him. He smelled so good to her - clean, woodsy and manly. She hoped he'd wake up soon so they could make love again. The only thing she wanted was to be as close to him as possible. The only way that was going to happen was if he was inside of her again. The thought of it made her ache with wanting him and she found that even though he was asleep, he was ready for her. She knew he'd awaken soon and then she'd have what she longed for. Kat turned in his arms, her back now facing him, and as Nick turned towards her, she found that she fit perfectly in that nook he created for her. The hard length protruding from him nestled between her legs and a smile lit her lips. She closed her legs around him and felt the throbbing emanating from him as he moved her hair aside and kissed the back of her neck. A shiver of delight ran through her as she anticipated what would come next. Those warm wet kisses wended their way down her back as Nick placed his hand in the sensitive area between her legs. He penetrated her with his fingers and she arched her back, throwing her head back on the pillow. Nick lifted her leg and drew her onto her back, finding that oh so sensitive nub that controlled her desire. She rode his hand as he now kissed her belly and reached up to caress her breast with his other hand. Her senses were being overwhelmed from all directions. She moaned and licked her lips. She longed to touch him and have him feeling what she was feeling. Her hands went to his hair, his beautiful brown curls, perfectly tussled and resting on her abdomen.

"We're doing this my way this time, lass," Nick uttered between kisses which had now reached her thighs.

"Mmm…" It felt so good she wanted to sink deeper and deeper into it and with Nick's help she did. He stroked, kissed, licked and loved her into a sensual haze that had her on the edge, ready to tumble down into euphoria. He held her hands at her side to keep them from interfering with what he was doing to her. She could feel the smile on his lips as they met the warmth of her core. He knew what he was doing and he knew it was good. She was at the point where she almost couldn't stand it a moment longer and why should she. She let herself go and felt the burst of warmth jerk through her body, leaving her heart pounding and her lungs gasping for air. And then he was atop her and inside of her, moving, moving and hitting every sensitive spot she never knew she had. He buried his face in her neck, his hands roving across her body and around to grasp her backside. He pulled her closer so he could dive deeply into her core and then with a few quick bursts he released himself within her as she joined him on their free fall from on high.

A knock at the door the following morning woke them. Kat glanced shyly in Nick's direction. He nodded to her that it was all right as he called, "Come in."

"Sir, Laird Sinclair asked that I bring ye both something to break yer fast." The servant carried in a tray of food and drink, which she left on the table at the foot of the bed.

"Thank you and thank Laird Sinclair for his thoughtfulness."

The lass left the room, softly closing the door behind her.

"Are ye hungry, love?" Nick leaned over and kissed her nose.

"Starving." Kat sat up and held the fur skin throw up across her breasts.

Nick rose from the bed, unconcerned by his nakedness and noted Kat's eyes following him.

"Just what do ye think yer looking at, lass?"

Kat giggled. "I'm looking at a very nice backside. It was dark last night. I really couldn't see you, but now in the light of day…"

"I hope yer not disappointed," Nick teased as he came around to her side of the bed carrying her shift, which had ended up on the floor. He gently placed it over her head and waited for her to finish dressing. He helped her up and then wrapped a fur around her as he led her to a seat by the table.

"Not disappointed at all. I like what I see," Kat returned with a mischievous grin.

They shared the food in between kisses. Nick had never in his entire life felt this way about anyone. He was under Kat's spell and happy to be there.

"Kat, I want you to know something." He had his serious face on again. "I wanted to woo you properly, but alas things didnae happen that way. I hope ye dinnae mind."

"You're sweet. I don't mind at all. It happened just the way I would've wanted it to."

"Truly?"

"Yes, truly."

"Kat I don't know when it happened, or how it happened, but I've fallen completely and hopelessly in love with you. I hope that in time ye'll come to love me as well, but for now I'd be happy if ye'd agree to be me wife."

Kat appeared startled by his declaration of love, which worried him.

He furrowed his brow and cast an earnest gaze her way. "I understand if ye dinnae wish to be me wife."

"Nick, wait. Don't jump to conclusions. I was just savoring what you said. You don't have to wait for me to love you."

Nick cocked his head to the side in confusion.

"You don't have to wait, because I already love you.

I don't know how or when it happened either, but somehow I feel like it was just meant to be."

"So, will ye marry me," he could hardly contain himself. If she said nay it would be hard to live with, but what choice would he have?

"I will. I will marry you, Nick. It would be my honor to marry you."

Nick almost fell to the floor in relief, but he managed to stay in his seat.

"Ye've made me the happiest man on earth, lass."

"Would you care to go riding with me this morning, Kat?" Nick was getting dressed as Kat continued enjoying the warmth of the bed she'd climbed back into right after eating.

"The last thing I want to do today is get on the back of a horse. It seems I've done nothing but ride continuously since I've arrived in your time." Kat yawned and stretched, sticking a leg out from the covers testing the air temperature in their chamber. Seeing Nick's disappointment at her response, she said "I'd much rather go for a walk with you." She'd really rather he climb back into bed with her, but she knew that wouldn't be appropriate as they were guests of Laird Sinclair and while they had his blessing to spend the night together, she doubted it would be considered right from them to stay in bed all day.

Nick's obvious disappointment faded at her suggestion. "Ye'd best rise then, m'lady. Our host must be wondering where we are." He grabbed her clothes up from the floor and dropped them on the foot of the bed. It was apparent he recognized her reluctance to leave the comfort of the bed. "Here, I'll help ye get dressed. We'll do it quickly so ye dinnae get cold."

Kat realized she was a very lucky lady. Nick would take good care of her. He'd already shown her he would in so many ways. She giggled as he worked, first getting her undergarments in place and then her gown, all the while teasing and tickling her. She loved this playful side of Nick. He always made things seem more fun and exciting and they really were when she was with him.

When Kat was fully dressed they made their way down to the great hall, which was no longer being occupied by Laird Sinclair or any of the men. Kat and Nick had spent too much time in their chamber and missed the opportunity to visit with their host.

"We'll see him at the noon meal," Nick assured Kat.

They'd decided to stay at Sinclair Castle for a few more days. Nick wanted to give Kat the time she needed to recover from the ordeal she'd just endured. He put her cloak on and guided her towards the door. "'Tis been some time since I've been to this castle. Many, many years. I ken 'tis cold outside, so we willnae stay out long, but it would be good for ye to see Sinclair castle in this time. I ken ye've seen it as a ruin in the future."

"I'd like that very much. Whenever I was out on an archeological site, I always wondered about what things would have looked like in their appropriate time. I'm excited to see more of it than I've glimpsed so far." They had reached the doors now and headed out into the courtyard, which was filled with activity. Water was being drawn from the well for use in the kitchen, sparks were flying from the black-smith's shop, stone masons were busy creating blocks of stone which would be used in the walls of an outbuilding that was being construct-ed. It was fascinating to Kat and she drank it all in. "It's so much nicer to see Castle Sinclair as it should be, filled with people and activity, instead of barely standing and silent.

"What was your life like there," Nick asked.

"You mean in the future?" she looked to Nick and he nodded. "Lonely." That was the only word that came to mind and the sad expression on Nick's face told her that she needed to explain. "It wasn't a bad place to be. It was just that being an orphan I had no one I could really rely on. I spent a good deal of time alone, except when I was working, but even then It was more about getting the job done than meeting people."

"So ye have no idea who yer Ma and Da were? 'Tis a shame. I be-lieve they'd be most proud to call ye daughter if they'd been able to see the woman ye've become." Nick warmed her hands in his.

"As I've been told, I was found on a street in Edinburgh. Actually it was more like an alley. Whenever I was in Edinburgh I'd go back to see the spot where I was left. I don't know why. I guess maybe I was hoping that I'd find my mother or father there, looking for me. It's silly, I know."

"Not at all, Katriona." He pulled her close and kissed her head.

"Well, from there I was put in foster care and I never stayed in one place for very long. As a matter of fact, within the first year I ended up in London. The families I was placed with were always very nice, but I never truly felt at home with any of them. I never caused them a bit of trouble or worry, unlike some of the others in their care. Even still, no one wanted to adopt me and the older I got, the less likely that became, until I found myself of legal age and out on my own. I had to make my own life and I did. I earned a degree in arche-ology and got a job working for Malcolm Granger."

"Were ye ever in love," Nick asked. The expression on his face was adorable. She could see he wanted to know, but he was hoping the answer would be no.

"No. I was too busy working out in the field to meet anyone. The people I spent the most time with were other archeologists. I went on a few dates here and there." Kat glanced up at Nick to see if he understood what she was saying, but she could tell he did. He'd lived in San Francisco for two years, so she didn't need to explain. "It was awkward dating people I had to see at work the next day, so after a while I didn't bother."

"If ye found the emerald, Kat, would ye want to go back?" He seemed to be holding his breath, awaiting her answer.

"I could never leave you. This is where I belong now, here with you. I wouldn't want to go back, I can promise you." She squeezed his hand and rested her head on his arm. She really meant it. This was her home now. It felt like home, unlike anyplace she'd ever lived before and she was anxious to get her life as a Mackall started.

After their walk, they returned to the castle to find Aleck striding purposefully back into the great hall.

"Aleck," Nick called to him.

Aleck spun to greet them, an expression of surprise on his face. "There ye be. I wasnae expecting to see either of ye fer quite some time."

Kat felt her face turning red at his knowing glance in her direction. "I wanted to see the castle grounds, so Nick and I went for a walk. It's quite beautiful."

"Thank ye, lass. I'm happy ye approve." He motioned for them to follow him, which they did. He brought them to a smaller room with a roaring fire and pointed towards the chairs. "Sit. Please. I'll send fer some warm cider." He went to the door and yelled into the passageway. "Eldred! Bring warm cider fer meself and me two guests." Closing the door, he turned back to Nick and Kat. "How are ye today, Katriona?" He seemed genuinely concerned.

"Relieved to be away from those two madmen." At his smile, she said "I don't believe I could feel any better." She glanced Nick's way and caught him smiling softly at her.

"And what of ye, Nick?" Aleck sat in a chair opposite them.

"I'm happy to be here with Kat safe by me side and in such good company as yerself."

The door opened and Eldred brought in a tray which he set on a nearby table. "Yer cider, sir."

"Thank ye, Eldred, ye can go." Aleck rose and went to the table where he poured the cider, handing one to Kat and one to Nick before pouring for himself.

Kat saw Aleck as a very handsome, strong and capable leader for his clan. She assumed if he had a wife they would have been introduced by now, but if he didn't she wondered why he wasn't already taken. "Aleck, I hope you don't mind me prying, but is there a woman in your life?"

Aleck chuckled and winked at her. "No, at least not anyone I'd spend the rest of me days with."

"Why is that? I can't believe there's no one out there that wouldn't want to be your wife." Kat sipped her cider and observed him over the rim of her cup.

"'Tis nae that I've not caught the eye of many a neighboring laird. I've nae found a woman who I felt was right for me. Right to be me partner here at Castle Sinclair. When she presents herself, I'll ken it, but until then I am happily on my own."

"I have two sisters in need of a husband," Nick offered.

"And I would love to be introduced to them, although ye ken I can only marry one," Aleck laughed.

"We'll have to arrange fer ye to meet them. Perhaps when ye come to visit with us." Nick smiled warmly at his host.

Kat could tell Nick appreciated Aleck's good humor, but she also knew that as laird of the Mackalls it would be his duty to find husbands for his sisters. "They're both beauties, Aleck." She wanted to help. Aleck shouldn't be alone and neither should Nick's sisters.

Merry was as sweet and innocent as could be and Isla was more of a challenge. It was the difference between a sunshiny day and a cloudy one. For some reason Kat felt Isla would be the better match for Aleck, but she kept her opinion to herself. It wasn't up to her to make that decision.

"I'll commit to coming to Dunaill, but I cannae commit to marrying anyone until I've gotten to know them and love them. I'm sure ye understand." He directed his last comment to Nick.

"Of course. I want me sisters to be happy and in order for that to happen, I believe it best that they love the men who will be their husbands."

"We're in agreement then," Aleck stood and placed his cup on the table. "I've some things to attend to, but I want ye both to feel free to explore Castle Sinclair to yer hearts delight."

"Thank you, Aleck," Kat said. "I love exploring old…" She caught herself. She'd almost said old castles.

Aleck didn't appear to notice as he was already heading out the door. "I'll see ye this evening."

They sat in silence, sipping their cider for a few moments longer. "I almost slipped and said the wrong thing." Kat stood and worriedly paced back and forth.

"He didn't notice, love. All is well." Nick stood and pulled her into his arms for a hug.

"I know. I'm just afraid I'm going to do or say the wrong thing to the wrong person and then I'll be in big trouble."

"Don't worry. We'll do our best to explain everything when we get back home. Me family willnae be a problem, but as for any others, we'll have to be careful. I'll be there to help ye." He chucked her under the chin and she relaxed, a sweet smile spreading across her face.

"Can we explore some more, Nick?" She really wanted to see the inside of the castle, especially the places she'd excavated before being transported to this time.

"Aye. Lead the way, love. I'm happy to follow ye where ever ye may wish to take me." He gave her a playful swat on her bottom as she began to walk away. "I like the view from back here, I believe I'll let ye do all the leading from this point forward."

She turned to him, rolling her eyes as she did, and took his hand. "Behave yourself."

"Easier said than done, lass." He had that mischievous look in his eyes again. "I believe there were some things upstairs in our chambers that we havenae explored yet."

Nick was sure to see that every one of Kat's needs was being met, both inside and outside of their chambers. They went for daily walks and as she had shared her true past with him, he shared his with her. She wanted to know all about his time in San Francisco and said on more than one occasion how wonderful it would have been if they'd met in that future time. Today he'd convinced her to get on her horse and join him for a ride around Sinclair lands.

"I ken ye dinnae wish to ride, but it would be best to ride at least a little today, as tomorrow we'll be on our horses all day. I dinnae wish fer ye to be uncomfortable on our journey." If it were within his power, he would magically transport her back to Dunaill to save her from the weary journey ahead.

"Where are we going?" she asked as he gave her a leg up on her horse.

"There's a loch nearby. I remember it being quite beautiful in the spring and summer, but I've nae seen it in winter." He directed their horses through the gates of Sinclair castle and followed the road that led them through a row of crofter's cottages and then to a tree-lined path decorated with snowy branches that gave it an enchanted quality.

"This is so pretty, Nick! I love it!" Kat appeared genuinely enthralled by the magic of the forest path they followed.

On the path itself, the snow had been trodden down to a manageable level by carts and horses that had ridden over it in recent days. It hadn't snowed again since they'd been at Castle Sinclair and Nick hoped the weather remained fair for their travel back to Dunaill.

"Are ye ready to leave tomorrow, Kat?" If she said no, then they would delay their departure until she felt up to making the trip.

"Yes. Very much so. I can't wait to get back." She appeared thoughtful. "Not that I haven't enjoyed staying here. Everyone at Castle Sinclair has been so nice, Aleck especially."

"I believe ye've earned a special place in his heart." Aleck seemed to have taken a keen interest in Kat, but Nick wasnae jealous at all. Aleck's interest was more that of a brother or father. He was concerned for her well being and Nick found that quite touching. Kat had a way of finding her way into the hearts of everyone she met, except of course those who didn't have a heart.

"That's nice. I like him a lot too." They rounded a bend in the road and Kat gasped, putting her hands to her mouth in delight. "Nick!"

"Aye. I see it, Kat." The lake was completely frozen over and the trees surrounding it were covered with a mixture of snow and icicles. A small creek which fed the lake, was off to their left and covered in ice itself, which led to a frozen waterfall.

"It's breathtaking. I can't seem to find the words to describe how I'm feeling right now." Kat stopped her horse and sat scanning from left to right and back again. "Thank you so much for sharing this with me." She smiled warmly in his direction.

"I cannae take credit for its beauty, but I'd do anything within my power to make ye this happy always." He moved Laoch closer to Kat and took her hand. They sat drinking in the lake in all its winter finery.

"Ye ken I'll be spending all me time searching out places such as this to take yer breath away, love."

Kat glanced lovingly in his direction, shaking her head. "We'll find them together."

20

Happiness was hard to come by and even harder to hold onto. So while she was ecstatic this morning to be heading back to Dunaill, there was a hint of worry that it could all be taken away from her in a heartbeat. Kat had lived her whole life not expecting happiness. It wasn't that she was unhappy, but she had always lived her life on the outside looking in. She wanted family and traditions but because she never stayed in one place for very long, those things didn't happened for her.

She gazed lovingly at Nick as he organized the men in the courtyard. They were going home today. Home. Her new home, far away from all the things she'd become accustomed to - cell phones, computers, cars, modern conveniences. The funny thing was, she'd never really cared about all that stuff, because that's all it was - stuff. She could live without it as long as she had her man by her side. She was not only gaining a husband and partner, but for the first time in her life she was getting a family. Good people who would be there for her through thick and thin. She smiled thinking about it.

"Are ye ready, love?" Nick was at her side, lifting her chin in his hand.

"More than you could possibly know."

He tipped his head and cocked an eyebrow in question, but then leaned down to kiss her cheek. "Idris is saddled and waiting for ye. Come, let's say goodbye to our host." He took her hand and led her to a gathering of men near the horses. Aleck Sinclair could clearly be seen in their midst. His shining blonde locks cascaded down past his shoulders and his hearty laugh could be heard as they approached. Nick placed a hand on his shoulder and Aleck turned to face them.

"Thank ye for yer kindness, Aleck. If ye find yerself near Dunnet Head or ye'd like to come and stay fer a while, we'd be happy to see ye and will surely return your hospitality."

"Are ye planning to marry this lovely lass," Aleck asked. That mischievous twinkle showing in his eyes, and dimples formed in his cheeks as he smiled.

"Aye. I've asked her and she's said yes. Will ye come to the wedding?"

"I thought ye'd never ask. Of course I will."

"My dearest Katriona, it has been a pleasure having ye here with us. Ye are always welcome."

"Thank you, Aleck." Katriona felt a fondness for him from the moment she'd met him. He was younger than Nick, and perhaps even a year or two younger than Kat, but he had a fatherly way about him, or at least she imagined he did. There was something familiar and warm about him, something she couldn't quite place, but she felt the urge to hug him and so she did.

Aleck seemed a bit surprised at first, but almost immediately wrapped her in a warm embrace. "Ye take good care of the lass, Nick. If ye dinnae, ye'll have me to answer to." He released his hold on her and Nick immediately took her hand and began to draw her away.

They all said their goodbyes and made promises to see each other again soon. Nick gave Kat a leg up to her horse and she smiled brightly at Aleck. Why did she suddenly feel sad about leaving him? It was odd. So many people had come and gone in her life she'd learned early on not to get attached. This feeling was unusual and she didn't seem to have any control over it. Tears pricked at her eyes and she quickly brushed them away. It was obviously due to the ordeal she'd just experienced. Of course, she was grateful to Aleck for his part in helping her.

They rode out of the gates and began their journey back to Dunaill. They took the faster route as Nick told her he couldn't wait to get her back home to the family. Duncan rode up beside her and gifted her with a warm smile. "How do ye fare, sister? Be sure to let us know if ye tire. We can stop at any time ye need."

"Thank you, Duncan." He'd called her sister. She'd always wanted to be somebody's sister. Maybe this time the happiness she was feeling wouldn't be fleeting.

Maybe she'd finally come to the place she was meant to be. Maybe this was her happily ever after.

"Duncan, I think I can take care of me betrothed.

Dinnae ye have anything else to occupy yer time?" Nick said.

"Brother, 'tis nae that I believe ye cannae care for Katriona, but at times ye are so focused on what yer about that ye forget everyone else around ye."

"Is that so? How could I possibly forget about ye when yer always reminding me of yer presence with yer incessant talking?"

Kat couldn't help but giggle. She could see that this was normal banter for the brothers. They seemed to take pride in one-upping each other. To prove the point, Duncan winked at her and laughing, turned his horse back to ride alongside the others.

"Dinnae mind Duncan," Nick said, smiling as he gazed into her eyes.

"I don't mind at all," Kat replied. "I like your brother. He's a good man."

"Aye. He is. But dinnae tell him what ye think.

He'll be reminding me of it always." Nick scanned the trees they were riding through. "Would ye care to stop, love?"

"I'm fine for now. We can keep going." She sat up taller in her saddle, signaling that she was ready and willing to go as far as he felt necessary in their day of riding.

Nick gazed lovingly at her and Kat wanted to jump out of her saddle and into his arms. A memory of his holding her close against his chest came to her from the night before and she held onto it.

"Why are ye smiling?" Nick asked, apparently noting her dreamy grin.

"Just thinking about you and about last night."

He didn't answer her right away and she noticed him shifting uncomfortably in his saddle.

"Ye've created an image in me mind that I willnae be able to remove until I have you in me arms again." "I like the sound of that," she teased.

"We'll nae have a bed to sleep in tonight, love.

We'll be forced to sleep among the men."

She understood what he was saying and while she was disappointed that they wouldn't make love again tonight, she would be happy just sleeping next to him, feeling safe and loved. She let her gaze rest on him. He was so handsome. Brown tousled curls, tawny eyes, muscular build. She'd better think about something else or she really was going to jump from her horse to his.

As she scanned the area around them, she thought she saw a party of small elfin creatures making their way through the woods alongside of them, but when she tried to focus on them she saw nothing. This happened over and over again, playing with her sense of reality. Who were they and why couldn't she focus on them? She began to watch them from the corner of her eye and was surprised that she could make out miniature horses carrying a party of miniature people. At the head of the group sat a woman, dressed in fine emerald-green velvet. Her cape was lined with soft fur and what Kat could see of her face was beautiful. Behind her rode about ten men, dressed like their much larger counterparts riding in Kat's party.

"Nick," she began to speak hesitantly. She didn't want him to think she'd lost her mind. "Do you see anything out of the ordinary?"

"Nae. Why? What do ye see?" He alertly began to search the trees for whatever she was talking about.

"It's probably nothing, but I could swear there's a group of little people following us. No. Actually riding alongside us, but just over there." She pointed to the empty path beyond the trees.

"Kat. I see nothing at all. Are ye feeling all right?"

"Yes. When I look straight at them, I can't see them either, but try looking out of the corner of your eye."

Nick gave her a strange look, but did as she asked.

She watched as he stiffened in his saddle. He'd seen them.

"You see them, don't you?"

"Aye. 'Tis the elves yer seeing. Their queen, Anania, is leading them. "What do they want?" he whispered.

"I don't know, but they've been there for a while now. I thought I was seeing things, because every time I tried to get a good look, they disappeared."

"We'll continue on to our campsite. If they wish us to see them, they will make themselves known to us at that time."

Nick seemed pretty sure about that. "How do you know that?"

"I don't. But it seems they are riding with us, although on another plane."

Kat thought about that for a moment. "Another plane?

Like another dimension?" She thought that was what he meant, but wanted to clarify it.

"Aye. Another dimension. Ye ken now that I wasnae making things up when I spoke of faeries. They too are real and they live here in these woods."

"Okay. I guess where I'm from they're not around anymore."

"Or perhaps they're just nae visible to those who dinnae believe."

"If that's true, then why can I see them? I'm not a believer in folklore."

"Mayhap Anania has a message fer ye and kens that ye'd receive it now that ye've experienced that which is without explanation. We'll find out soon, I believe.

Nick kept their pace up for the rest of the day. They stopped just long enough to eat, rest and water their horses. As they arrived at their campsite, Nick cast his gaze around in search of the elves who'd been their constant companions that day. They were no longer visible.

He watched as Kat spun around in search of them also, but not finding them she returned to his side and held onto his arm. "I don't see them anywhere."

"Nay. They may be nearby, but we'll have to wait for them to come to us. Dinnae fear. They willnae harm us."

"How do you know that?"

"'Tis a feeling I have. No matter. I will protect ye should the need arise." His eyes sparked with humor as he said, "I think ye should stay right by me side just in case."

She wrinkled her nose at him and he laughed. She was precious to him in so many ways. He wouldnae disappoint her - his woman, his love.

The men were gathering firewood and building a fire.

They placed some larger logs around the fire to sit on and Nick ushered Kat to one. He sat beside her and Duncan joined her on her other side. She suddenly felt tiny sitting as she was between two very tall and braw men. They watched as the others finished making camp and then all found their way to the fire. One of the men, Alan, broke out his griddle and they collected food from the saddlebags which he expertly prepared.

Rory retrieved a rebec from his pack and began to play while they waited to eat. To Kat's eyes it looked like a small pear shaped violin and sounded similar as well. The men began to sing a song that sounded familiar to Kat, although she couldn't place how she knew it.

It brought her back to a time when she was very young, but that was all she knew. She had no memories from those early days. She was found by a passerby on a street in Edinburgh, just a baby. She wished she knew more, but it didn't seem important anymore. She'd found the life she was supposed to live. It took longer than she could have imagined, but now that she had it she refused to let it go.

Food was passed around the fire and everyone had a good-sized portion. No one was going hungry in this group. They were prepared for travel, having done it often Kat imagined. She daintily ate her food, while the men around her practically inhaled theirs. The men sat and conversed quietly, laughter occasionally drifting into the air along with the smoke from their fire.

"Where do you suppose they've gone?" Kat asked Nick.

"The elves? They, like us, are taking the time to nourish themselves and to rest. I dinnae believe we'll see them again tonight."

"I couldn't see her face clearly; what do you think she looks like?"

"I couldnae say, love. The elves are quite fair of face. I would venture to guess that she is verra beautiful. She is their queen after all."

Kat covered her mouth and yawned. "I'm getting sleepy."

Some of the others were already bedding down near the fire. Nick stood and offered her his hand. He went to his saddle and removed a plaid to place beneath them and another to cover them as they slept. Kat had no doubt she would sleep well and Nick would keep her warm.

Kat snuggled into the warmth created by Nick's body. He was sleeping soundly, as were the rest of the men. She, however, was wide awake, when earlier she'd felt exhausted. As she stared across the fire at the clearing beyond, she saw movement in the trees. She froze, frightened of what or who may be approaching. As she watched, a beautiful redheaded woman gracefully walked towards her. The elven queen, Anania, was approaching and Kat wasn't sure whether to hide beneath the plaid or to greet her. She elbowed Nick, but he didn't wake.

"I've caused your men to sleep deeply, Katriona. Do not fear me. I mean you no harm." Anania sat on one of the logs near the fire. "Join me. I have much to tell you."

Kat stood and walked towards her. Anania waved an arm and covered Kat with a warm fur blanket. Kat was grateful and said as much.

"Of course, my dear. I dinnae wish ye to be cold." Anania smiled warmly at her. "I imagine yer wondering why I've come to speak with ye."

Kat nodded as her voice seemed to be hiding.

"Yer not who ye believe yerself to be, lass. Before ye were born, yer mother made a pact with me. She agreed to give up her first-born daughter and I would see to it that she gave birth to an heir."

Kat was puzzled and must have looked it, because Anania took her hand. "Fear not, Katriona. I willnae tell ye anything that ye dinnae already feel deep down inside. Ye are back where ye belong, among yer own people."

"I'm not sure what you're talking about. I'm from a different time."

"That is what ye believe, but 'tis nae the way of it. I sent ye to the future when ye were a babe. I wished to protect ye and the people of Scotland from Ariweth, an evil sorcerer who would have stolen ye away for his own evil purposes. Yer mother didnae wish to leave ye go, but she understood that it was best for ye and the people. I promised her next child would be a lad. She resigned herself to losing ye. Dinnae ever doubt that she loved ye, because she made the ultimate sacrifice for yer safety, but still she cried herself to sleep every night at yer loss."

"But why did this sorcerer want me?" She wasn't important to anyone; she didn't understand how she fit into this whole scenario.

"He thought that if he kidnapped ye, yer family would help him attain what he wanted most in this world. Ye ken the sword that yer Granger fellow wanted. Ariweth created it to destroy the Scottish royal family by making King James his puppet and forcing him to carry out his evil plans. When he found that the Pope was gifting King James with a sword, he made his sword, the Twin Sword, an exact replica. When James opened the gift from the Pope, he was surprised to find two swords that were exactly the same, with the exception of the engraving along the blade. A note from Ariweth, promising James unlimited power to rule the world, confirmed his suspicions about the sword. He knew immediately that it shouldnae be used. He tried destroying it, but no matter how they tried, they couldnae. So he made the decision to hide it away where no one could ever retrieve it. I did my part by sending ye to the future and then removing a piece of it that wouldnae allow him what he wished. The green emerald he had embedded in the sword was the seed of its power and without it, he was unable to accomplish his goal and with his power greatly diminished, I trapped him in a place where his powers, or what's left of them, are almost completely useless. Still he managed to call Granger, a kindred spirit, to him from the future. And while he could not bring the emerald into his prison, he was able to place it where ye would find it, forcing yer return with it here."

"What if he'd gotten hold of it? What would have happened?"

"There was never a chance he would get his hands on that emerald. As soon as it crossed the plane into this time, I was aware of its presence. Ye dropped it when ye arrived and it sat in the field near Castle Sinclair. He was not satisfied to let the emerald or ye go. He sent Granger to retrieve ye both. Ye ken the rest."

Kat ruminated on what she'd just heard. So her life in the twenty-first century was all an awful sham. She was never meant to live her life there, but Ariweth made it impossible for her to stay with her family. "Ye say I have a brother."

"Aye. Did ye nae recognize him?" Anania scooted a bit closer to Kat.

"Recognize him? Ye mean I've met him?" Kat was astonished to hear this.

"Ye did. Although ye dinnae ken it, I believe ye had a connection with this man." She tipped her head, apparently waiting for Kat to catch on.

"Wait a minute. You mean, Aleck Sinclair is my brother?" Joy bubbled up in her and came out in a giggle. "I knew there was something about him that felt familiar to me. I thought it was just that he helped to save me."

"Aye. He felt it too."

"So, I'm a Sinclair?" Kat almost jumped from the log she was seated on, so great was her excitement.

Anania smiled and nodded.

"I have to tell him. I have to tell Nick." This time she did hop up from her seat.

Anania rose as well, taking Kat's hands in hers. "I have something for ye, lass. Placing a velvet bag in Kat's hands, she said, "Open it!" Kat did as she was directed and was shocked to see the emerald in the palm of her hand. She panicked, nearly dropping it, but Anania grasped her hands and gazed reassuringly into her eyes. "Dinnae fear. Yer not going back. Unless, of course, ye wish to."

"No. I want to stay." Kat didn't even hesitate. "This is where I belong, with Nick." She continued eyeing the emerald in her hand.

"Good. I'm happy to hear it. Ye ken the emerald doesnae have the power to transport ye, so ye need nae fear it," Anania reassured her.

"But if the emerald didn't bring me back, what did?" "Ariweth. He used the emerald as a lure. As soon as ye had it in yer hand he knew and brought ye back." "But why are you giving it to me?"

"It is yours to protect. Keep it with ye always and let nae other possess it. As long as ye hold it in yer possession, Ariweth cannae get to it. It holds no power on its own, only when combined with the sword. Remember, if ye ever wish to go back to yer home in the future, ye only need to call on me and I'll see to yer safe return." She gazed at Kat with a questioning look.

"Now that I know the truth, I could never go back there. Everything I've ever dreamed of or wanted is right here and I'm never going to leave." She was adamant about that.

"As ye wish, lass." Anania waved her hand, one over the other, and a cup appeared. "I will leave ye now, but before I go, I would have ye drink this draught. After all ye've learned tonight, it will help ye to sleep." She handed it to Kat, who looked unsure. "Dinnae fear.

It will nae harm ye."

Kat lifted the cup to her lips and drank and when she was done, Anania was gone.

21

Was it all a dream, or had she really spoken with Anania. She didn't remember climbing back into Nick's arms and when she awoke she questioned everything. Was she really Aleck's sister? Was she really born in this time and not the twenty-first century? What if it was all true? And the scary part was that this evil sorcerer had somehow pulled her into his plot to take over the Scottish throne. The velvet pouch clutched in her hands answered all her questions.

"Nick! Nick, wake up!" She shook him and he slowly opened those mesmerizing eyes of his. "Nick something strange has happened."

"Come back to sleep, love," Nick's voice, thick with sleep touched a chord deep inside.

"As much as I'd love to, I have to tell you something."

"What could have happened in the short time you've been awake that's so important you would rob me of my last few moments of sleep," he teased.

"Seriously, Anania was here last night. She spoke with me. I wasn't sure if it was a dream or if it was true until now." She had his attention now.

Nick sat up and wrapped his plaid around them both. The fire had died down during the night and one of the men was up and trying to bring it back to life.

"I was sleeping when something woke me. I saw her standing there and she beckoned me to join her by the fire. She said I'm not from the future, that my place is here. I was born here in this time and, and…"

"Anania said you were born in this time… not the future?"

"Yes, and I know it's all true because she gave me this." She opened the bag and dropped the emerald into her palm.

Nick quickly grabbed hold of her. "No, dinnae go!" "Don't worry, Nick. I could hold his emerald in my palm all day and never go anywhere. The emerald isn't what brought me here. It was Ariweth." She put the emerald back in the bag and gave Nick a quick, happy peck on the lips.

Nick smiled lovingly at her, but obviously still had questions. "And what else? What else did she tell ye?"

"Aleck is my brother."

"What?" Nick appeared thoughtful. "Now that I think on it, ye do share a resemblance."

Kat told him the rest of the story. Everything Anania had told her from beginning to end. It was an incredible story and she was having a difficult time wrapping her brain around it. "Can you believe it?"

"Aye. I can and I do. As strange as it seems, there was a reason she rode along with us yesterday and now it all makes sense. I knew ye were special from the moment I first laid eyes on ye."

"My whole life I thought I was alone and that I had no family, but to find out I've had one all along is the best gift I could receive, that and meeting you of course."

Nick gently kissed the tip of her nose. "Ye must be elated," he observed. "We have much to do when we arrive home. We must arrange for our marriage and our celebration and we must send word to yer brother. He will come for the wedding and ye can get to know each other better."

"It's like a dream, all of it."

"Did Anania tell ye what she plans for Ariweth.

Surely she'll do something to keep him safely locked away wherever he is."

"Aye. She did. His powers have diminished steadily over the years, but he still retains some. She will continue to keep watch over him and the sword. She doesnae wish him to ever get his hands on it. The stone is mine now and as long as I have it, he will not be able to retrieve it. Without it, the sword is useless."

"For that we should all be grateful." Nick stood and gave Kat his hand. "Come, let's break our fast and then be on our way home."

"Yes. Home."

Dunaill seemed prepared for their return. Lettie was waiting for them with a huge smile on her face as they rode in.

"Yer back," she called.

"Aye. Did ye think I disappeared again?" Nick asked.

He dismounted and then helped Kat down.

"I'll nae be able to let ye leave me sight without worry, Nick." As they approached, she threw her arms around them both. "I'm happy to see ye both. Do ye have something to tell me?"

"Why do I feel ye already ken what we have to tell ye?"

"Me mother's intuition has been telling me from the moment ye first returned to us with Kat by yer side that ye were meant for each other. I sent Aidan off to the Bishop of Caithness and got the annulment that ye wanted, Kat. The Sheriff has arrested the man who sold ye to Laird Calhoun. So, yer free to marry me son."

Kat smiled brightly at her mother-in-law to be. "Thank you, Lettie, but Bearach Calhoun is no longer a threat to me or to anyone else.

They quickly explained everything that had happened while they were gone and Lettie breathed an obvious sigh of relief. "We can all rest easy now. Yer one of us."

"Aye. She will be officially as soon as we can arrange it. We must invite her family to join us." Nick could hardly contain his excitement.

"Family?" Lettie's curiosity seemed piqued by this statement. "I thought ye didnae have one."

"I do, actually. I made up the whole 'my family was killed by highwaymen' thing. I hope ye can forgive me. I was merely trying to protect myself. I just found out that I have a brother in Aleck Sinclair. I had no idea and he doesnae ken it yet, but I'll be telling him when he arrives for the wedding."

"What a strange turn of events," Lettie said.

"Ma, I have something to tell ye and the rest of the family. I havenae been truthful with ye about where I was for the last two years. It will also help explain the rest of the news that Kat has to tell ye."

"Oh, my. I'm afeared of what ye might say, but come, let's get ye both inside. I'll call a family meeting and we'll sit while ye tell us yer tale." Lettie seemed curious and apprehensive all at once.

They entered the castle and went straight to the great hall. Warm cups of cider were served while they waited for the rest of the family to join them.

"Well, whatever ye have to say cannae be too bad the way ye two are smiling at each other," Lockie said.

"Ye'll hear soon enough." Nick smiled sweetly at Kat.

The others entered the room. Nick's sisters ran to hug him and then Kat. The lads joined round the fire. Some sat, some stood, but they all were paying close attention to the tale Nick was telling them.

"When I told ye that I had been in a faerie kingdom for two years, I don't suppose ye believed me, now did ye?"

"Nicks sisters nodded and his brothers shook their heads."

"'Twas a rather tall tale ye told," Lockie said. "Where were ye really?"

"I spent the last two years in the future. The year 2014 to be exact, in a place called San Francisco, California. I survived there due to the kindness of the people I was lucky enough to befriend. They gave me a place to stay and a job to do and I made a good life for me self. I wasnae sure I'd ever see any of ye again and that was the only thing that saddened me. It was a great adventure and one I'll always remember, but I'm happy to be back here with all of ye and I'm even happier to have met me love, Katriona, who as unbelievable as it may seem, has spent her entire life in the future. The same time I found myself in, but here in future Scotland and London."

Mouths were agape and everyone seemed speechless. Finally, Aidan spoke, "Yer not making up another tall tale, are ye?"

"Nae. This one is verra, verra true. There are others here in Scotland who have come from the future and there are others who have gone to the future only to return back to their homes. I'm one of those lucky people, as is Kat. Ye see, she grew up an orphan and has returned to find she has a brother."

The questions started pouring forth like water sluicing down stream. Nick and Kat answered every one of them with a truthfulness that came across and left the others without question of their authenticity. Kat told of Anania and the green gem. Nick told them about the sword and Malcolm Granger. It was a tale that would be told for years and years to come as the Mackalls sat around their hearth.

The family agreed that it would be for the best to keep the stories about traveling to the future to themselves. It was surely something that would raise great concern among the other castle occupants and the villagers.

Wedding preparations were made and Lettie was having the best of times helping Kat with her dress and with the decoration of the great hall for the first Mackall wedding since her own. Invitations were sent to the neighbors who had just been with them to celebrate Nick's return and a verra special invitation was sent to Aleck Sinclair, who was in for quite a surprise upon his arrival.

Nick doted on Kat. Whatever she wished he would make it his quest to provide. She wasnae a selfish lass, so most of what she wished for was always fer someone else. Still, he wanted to spoil her and he did his best. They hadnae shared a bed since their return and he hoped the wedding day would approach faster, because all he wanted was to hold her in his arms and love her. Stolen kisses and passionate embraces only made him want her all the more, but he knew that anything good, and Kat was so much more than good, was worth waiting for.

In the cold of winter, the occasion of Nick and Kat's wedding was a warm and inviting event that everyone for miles around came to participate in. There was good food and drink, as well as music and dancing. The bride and her groom barely took their eyes from each other.

Aleck arrived two days before the ceremony and was ushered into the great hall, where he sat with Nick and Kat as he was told the story Anania had shared with Kat.

"I hadn't forgotten that I had an older sister who disappeared when she was just a bairn. We thought the fairies had taken her. 'Twas ye. I should have known. I felt a strange kinship with ye from the moment I first met ye. I'm the happiest of men to ken that I have a sister, and after this wedding a new brother. Our parents grieved yer loss for their entire lives. Mother had three more babies, who were all stillborn. After the last, she was exhausted and quickly fell ill. She left us to join all the little lost souls she'd tried to birth and who we thought to be with ye. Father and I muddled along without her, two lonely men in a big castle full of folk. Our father died a few short years ago, I wish ye could have come back before that time, so ye could've known him. They were good people. The salt of the earth."

Kat had tears in her eyes the whole time. Aleck stood and went to her, pulling her up from her seat and wrapping her in a bear hug. She sobbed into his chest and Nick had to wipe a tear or two from his own eyes.

Lettie peeked in from the passageway and she too was sniffling.

"Kat, we've lost many years, but now we've found each other. This is a joyous time for us all. No more tears. The past is behind us and from this moment on we have each other. You, who were so alone yer whole life, now have a brother and a new family to spend the rest of yer life with."

Wiping her eyes with her sleeve, Kat smiled up at her handsome younger brother. Love had finally filled her heart with a peace she'd never experienced before.

Life had always happened around her, but not to her and now she was experiencing all that life had to offer and she wanted to feel every bit of it. Her emotions had run the gamut from fear, to sadness, to love, to complete happiness. She was a verra, verra lucky lass by any standard.

She couldn't stop hugging Aleck. His warm brotherly love fed that place deep in her soul that needed it the most and she knew he was feeling it as well.

Nick might have been jealous of all the time she was spending with Aleck, but he understood how important it was for her to do so. He also knew that after the wedding, Aleck would be leaving to return to his own castle and then he'd have Kat all to himself for the rest of his life. It was something well worth waiting for. He had a new brother and friend in Aleck and they would see each other as often as possible. He had promised them both.

The day of the wedding arrived and it was as wonderful as Kat had imagined it would be. Her dress was beyond beautiful. The cream colored velvet was decorated with embroidered flowers. She wore a Mackall plaid across one shoulder and pinned at the opposite waist with a beautiful emerald brooch that was a gift from Lettie. This was her special day. She was to wed her man. The man she'd learned she could trust above all others. The man who touched her soul and made her knees weak just gazing on him. Nick Mackall was to be her husband. She felt like the luckiest woman on earth. Nothing could make this day more complete.

The ceremony was a simple one, but it was filled with the love that Nick and Kat shared. It would be obvious to anyone observing them that they were truly meant to be together. They exchanged their vows and were declared married to the cheers of the crowd. The celebrating began with a toast to the bride and groom by Aleck Sinclair.

"To my sister and her husband, who is now my brother. May they live and love for many, many years to come."

Everyone drank to the happy couple. Many more toasts were made and food and drink were overflowing. The musicians began to play and the dancing and singing began. This went on long into the night. The happy couple escaped to their chamber before it was all said and done and closed and locked the door behind themselves.

22

"Wife," Nick began after depositing Kat on their bed. "I never imagined a day would come when I would find the love of my life and then be lucky enough to marry her and spend all my days showing her how much she is loved. I intend to show ye well this night."

Kat couldn't help but giggle, but at the same time she tingled from her head to her toes with anticipation. "Husband, I am all yours and always will be. I cannot imagine what my life would have been like if I hadn't met you that day in the woods. Deep down inside, something told me that you were the man for me. I will spend the rest of my days loving you and I, too, intend to show ye well this night."

Kat stood on the bed and did a seductive striptease while Nick's eyes shone with obvious lust for her. He walked to the bed and pulled her towards him, burying his face in her belly and kissing her while she wrapped herself around him.

"It's been a long time and I am not a patient man." He let go of her to remove his own clothing. Piece by piece they flew to the far corners of the room. When he was done, Kat ran her hands over the hard planes of his muscular chest and arms. He was perfect in her eyes. She shivered in anticipation. Nick took her hand and guided her back down to the bed, where she lay waiting as he scanned her body from head to toe. He ran a hand up the inside of her leg, stopping short before reaching the place she wanted him to touch. He was teasing her. She licked her lips as he watched, knowing the effect it was having on him. He surprised her by leaping onto the bed and laying his body over her entire length. He growled into her neck sending goosebumps all along her naked body. "Are ye cold?" A legitimate question considering that she'd complained of the cold more often than not since she'd known him. "If ye are, dinnae fear, fer I intend to warm ye with the fire that burns deep inside of me at the thought of ye."

Softly seeking her lips, Nick kissed her. The intensity of those kisses grew as she responded to them. Their tongues mingled in a loving duel, hands explored familiar places, but with new intensity. Kat lifted her hips to Nick and he drove himself inside of her. A moan of pleasure escaped them both and they joined in the rhythmic dance that would lead them to the place they desired, though they wished to delay their arrival for as long as possible, enjoying the pleasurable sensations of their bodies touching at all of their most sensitive points. They'd made love before, but this time it was done with the knowledge that their love for each other made it a spiritual experience. It touched their bodies, their hearts, their souls. Nick repositioned them so that he sat with Kat facing him, her arms entwined around his neck and with his hands firmly grasping her ass, she rode him. Their gazes met and held, each watching the pleasure they were giving to the other.

They could see it in each others' eyes. Their movements quickened as they each sought their release and when it came, Nick let loose a growl of pleasure, matched by Kat's moans of ecstasy. When it was over, they sat as they were for some time, neither wanting to break the spell they'd woven. Nick didn't wish to leave the warmth of her silky core, so he carefully laid her back on the bed and rested atop her. Kat for her part held tight, not wanting him to move from her. Their lovemaking had been perfect for their first night as a married couple. Nick was bursting with the love he felt for Kat. "I love you, my sweet."

"And I love you, my trusted highlander."

Nick smiled at that. She trusted him. Those simple words meant the world to him. To be trusted was a matter of honor. To be trusted by the one you loved was an honor. He would continue to hold her trust like the precious gift that it was.

The wedding feast continued below stairs. Aleck was dancing with Nick's sister Isla. He enjoyed her saucy personality. She wasn't all sweetness and light like her sister, Merry. She was a challenge and he had always prided himself on accepting any challenge that came his way. This lass would be no different. It was unfortunate he would be leaving in a day or two. It could be months before he saw her again, but if it was meant to be, then it would be. For now he was just enjoying her company.

"I believe I need a rest. Would ye care for something to drink," Isla asked as she stepped back away from him.

"I would." He followed her to a table filled with drink, enjoying the view of her swinging backside as she walked.

Isla handed him a cup of ale and took one for herself. "How long do ye plan on being with us?" she asked.

"Only for another day or two. I must return home to attend to business."

"Yer a busy man are ye? I thought ye might want to stay to spend time with yer newly found sister."

"Aye. I would like to get to know her better, but that time will come. I hope she'll come to visit with yer brother some time soon. Ye could join them ye ken."

"I could, but I dinnae believe I will. Ye see, I'm a busy woman myself. There is much that I must do here at my home."

"Surely yer family could spare ye for a short while."

"Nae. I dinnae believe they can. Thank ye fer the dance," she said as she began to walk away.

Playing hard to get, Aleck thought to himself. "Lass, I dinnae believe I've done speaking with ye."

"Ye have."

He enjoyed her bluntness, though he could tell she played with him. "Very well then, I'll find another to dance with me then." Aleck turned and headed back to the others. He spied Merry standing by the far wall and made his way towards her. He never even glanced back to see where Isla was. Two could play that game. "Merry, why do ye stand here all alone? Would ye care to dance?"

Merry, true to her nature, smiled sweetly at him.

She was a lovely young lady, but unlike her sister, she didn't pique his interest. "I'd love to, sir."

Aleck swirled her onto the dance floor and past an angry-looking Isla. He smiled. She could pretend all she wanted that she cared not for him, but he knew differently. It was written all over her face. He made polite small talk with Merry and when the dance was done, he took it one step further. He felt a little badly about deceiving Merry with his true intentions. "Merry, would ye care to join me outside fer some fresh air."

Merry appeared a little apprehensive as she glanced in Isla's direction. "I thought perhaps ye'd be wanting to go fer a walk with my sister."

"Yer sister has no desire to spend more time with me." Aleck said as he gazed down into her sweet face. "'Tis just a walk, nothing more, I promise."

"All right then." Merry gently laid her hand on his arm and he guided her outside. From the corner of his eye he could see Isla stewing in her own juices. *Perhaps she'll learn a lesson from this,* he thought as he placed his plaid around Merry's shoulders and they disappeared from the room.

Isla couldn't believe it. That man was a bastard. He'd spent the entire evening flirting with her and dancing with her and now he was wooing her sister out in the courtyard. The nerve of him. She practically stamped her foot she was so angry. Isla was used to getting whatever she wanted. She knew she was a bit rough around the edges, but it had always worked for her in the past.

Aleck Sinclair had turned out to be the exception to that rule. She had turned him down and he simply walked away from her and to her baby sister. Merry was too trusting. She'd probably end up in a compromising position if Isla didn't do something about it. She picked up her skirts and hurried towards the door. No need for a cape, her boiling blood would keep her warm. She hit the cold air with steam pouring from her nostrils like a dragon on a quest. Where were they? She scanned the courtyard and could see no one. She heard what sounded like her sister giggling like a wee lass over near the stables. She hurried in that direction, sure she'd find Aleck with his hands and mouth all over poor Merry.

Reaching the stables without any sight of them, she cautiously opened the door, which creaked loudly on its hinges. The stable was dark, with the exception of a light coming from a stall at the far end. She crept towards it, listening closely. She could hear a deep manly chuckle and her sister's soft giggle, which only served to urge her forward. If she had thought at all about turning back, those sounds drove her on.

Finally at the stall door and not sure what she should do, she barged in and startled both Mary and Aleck, who were sitting in the midst of a litter of kittens.

"Isla, what a surprise. Won't ye join us?" Aleck had a self-satisfied grin on his face.

"What are ye two doing in here?" she stammered. "Isla, look, one of the stable cats has had kittens.

Aren't they the cutest little things?"

Isla took a deep breath. Whatever she thought was going on between her sister and Aleck, had thankfully turned into a very innocent adventure for Merry.

Merry held up one of the kittens to her sister. "She had them yesterday and I wanted to show Aleck. Do ye wish to hold one?" Merry asked.

"No. And ye shouldn't hold them either. Their mother willnae take kindly to it. She may scratch ye."

"She's fine," Merry said, pointing to the mother who was busy nursing the other kittens.

"Well, at the verra least, ye should let that one eat."

"Are ye angry with me, Isla?" Merry asked.

"Nae. I'm not angry with ye. I just wanted to be sure ye were all right. I saw that ye came out here with him." She nodded her head in Aleck's direction.

"Did ye think I would compromise yer sister's virtue, Isla? I ken ye've just met me, but I can promise ye that it was nae my intention to do anything improper."

"Well, see that ye dinnae." Isla was so embarrassed.

She had no idea how she was going to get out of this position she'd forced herself into. She stared off into the corner, when she suddenly found herself with a furry little grey kitten being held at her face.

"Here, take this one. Ye ken ye want to," Merry said.

Reluctantly, Isla took the kitten from her sister. "'Tis so soft," she said, finding herself enjoying the sensation of petting the little one.

"Come, sit down here with us," Aleck offered, patting the ground next to him.

Isla sat, but made sure it was close to her sister and not to that infuriating man. She continued to do her best to ignore him, but every time she caught a glimpse of him from the corner of her eye, he was smiling at her. "Here," she shoved the cat back in Merry's hands and rose. "I'm going back to the great hall. 'Tis warmer there."

"We'll come with ye, won't we Aleck?" Merry put the kitten back with its mother and stood, offering her hand to Aleck to help him up.

Standing and brushing the straw from his clothes, he opened the stall door and motioned for the sisters to go first. He followed along behind, whistling a happy tune. "What makes ye so happy?" Isla said, sounding a bit sharper than she'd wished.

"I dinnae ken. I'm just happy. 'Tis a beautiful night and I am in the company of two beautiful lassies. Why should I nae be happy?"

Isla harrumphed her way towards the castle. She wanted to kiss that smug smile right off of his handsome face, but maybe she'd do better to slap it.

Unfortunately, she had no reason to. He'd been a perfect gentleman to her sister and to her. Her little act of playing hard to get had backfired on her and now she felt like a fool. She'd never been one to accept defeat and she wasn't going to this time. Before he left, Aleck would be begging her for a kiss and she'd be sure he didnae get one.

The hall doors were open and the warmth created by a room full of people dancing and having a good time, combined with the fire in the hearth, was most welcome after their frigid walk outside. Aleck had gotten what he wanted - the satisfaction of seeing Isla thwarted in her efforts to make him the fool. He had no doubt she'd try again, but he was enjoying this. She'd be begging him for a kiss by the time he left and he'd have to think about whether or not she'd receive one.

The evening had stretched into the wee hours of the morning and while he thought he could continue to dance and drink until dawn, he was feeling the need for sleep. He slipped from the great hall and headed upstairs to his chamber with the hopes of a good night's sleep dancing in his head. He was sure that most of the castle would be sleeping late tomorrow, considering that they were still downstairs reveling in the celebratory feast they'd been a part of. As his feet hit the top of the landing, he noticed a slight figure just ahead of him. "Isla?" he asked. Darkness was making it difficult to see her.

"Aye."

"Are ye off to bed then?" "Aye."

"Sleep well. I'll see ye on the morrow." "If yer lucky," she retorted.

He couldn't help but chuckle at that one. She was working extra hard to make him think she didn't care.

"What are ye laughing at?"

"Ye. I ken what yer about, lassie. I've seen it before, so I recognize it. Ye may need to change yer tactics." He was at the door to his chamber, which he opened. Entering the darkened chamber, he found a taper, which he lit using one from the passageway. Closing the door behind him, he placed it by the bedside and began to remove his boots and the rest of his clothes.

Thoughts of feisty Isla came unbidden to his brain and his loins. He would have her, he'd made up his mind. He liked a woman with a little fight to her. Isla, however, seemed to have a lot of fight to her. He'd need to plan his next moves, much as he would plan an attack on an enemy army - cautiously.

The morning after the wedding feast found the castle near to silent. The servants barely made their way around the great hall, cleaning as they went. The happy couple would probably be abed fer days, as it should be. As fer the rest of the clan, they would recuperate today and then be about their business. Aleck was one of the few guests up and moving. He went to the stable to check on his horse. After giving him a good brushing and feeding him some oats from his pocket, he returned to the great hall where he was greeted by Lettie.

"Good morning to ye," she said. "Would ye care to join me? I've sent fer some food. Please come sit." She motioned to the seat next to her at the table.

"I am rather hungry. I hadn't planned on rising quite so early, but here I am."

"Early fer some, but 'tis probably close to noon.

Everyone seems to have had a fine time last night. There are few about at this hour. That is the telltale sign." Lettie smiled at him, putting him at ease. Aleck wasn't sure how much of last night's goings on she'd been aware of.

"I see that ye've taken a fancy to my Isla." Lettie said in the blunt manner he recognized as Isla's. "I have nae problem with ye courting her. She can be difficult, I'll warn ye. Many a man has left here with his tail between his legs. She needs a strong man. Do ye believe that would be ye?"

"I can see where Isla gets her directness from. I am verra attracted to yer daughter, but as ye say, she's a hard one. I believe I can win her heart, but it will take work on my part and I'm afraid that I'll be leaving here in another day or two fer me home. Any wooing would undoubtedly have to wait."

"I see. Well, don't give up on her. I believe she's just been holding out for the right man. Her father and I always believed that our children should marry fer love first and clan ties secondly."

"I would agree. Love is important." "Do ye think ye could love her?"

He smiled. If he didn't know better he'd think she was trying to get rid of her daughter. "'Tis too soon to tell, although she has piqued my curiosity. I'm a man who enjoys a challenge, so Isla may have met her match."

"I hope so. She's nae getting any younger and I'd like to see her settled."

"What of Merry?"

"Merry is a sweet young lass. She'll have nae trouble finding a man to marry. She's already been beset with offers. But, as I've said. I want them to love the men they marry."

"Well, I cannae make ye any promises, Lettie, but I do find yer daughter intriguing. You are welcome at my home any time ye like. I wouldnae complain if ye brought Isla with ye." Aleck smiled warmly at Lettie. He liked her. As a matter of fact, he liked the entire family and was verra happy that his long-lost sister had married a Mackall. They were family now and while they had long been friendly, an unexpected alliance had now been made and he for one looked forward to what that would bring.

23

"I'm so happy!" Kat exclaimed as she sat up in the bed and stretched her arms high overhead. A moment later she was shrieking loudly as Nick took the opportunity to tickle her under her arms.

"How happy are ye, lass?" he laughed. He stopped tickling and pulled her back down under the covers.

"Happier than I ever thought I could be and it's all because of you," Kat tapped his nose with her finger. "Thank you."

"There's no need to thank me, lass. I'm just doing me duty as a good husband." The twinkle of mischief she loved was shining in his eyes.

"I wasn't thanking you for *that*." Kat patiently explained.

Nick's mock look of shock had her giggling. "Then what were ye thanking me fer?"

"For finding me, for rescuing me, for loving me and for teaching me to trust again. I love you for all of that and so much more."

Nick got very serious. "I see. And my lovemaking is not something yer thankful for?" She could tell he was teasing her now.

"Did I mention making me laugh?" Kat was playing along now.

"And the lovemaking?" he repeated.

"Hmmm... I'm hungry; are we ever going to go downstairs to eat again?" She tried to get out of bed, but Nick had other ideas.

"Not until I make ye grateful fer me lovemaking!" He smothered her with kisses, which led to more kisses and then before they knew it they were both lying in tousled sheets, panting from the exhilaration.

"Alright! You win! Thank you for your lovemaking." Kat kissed his nose and rolled to the edge of the bed. "I'm getting up now."

"Finally. I thought I was going to have to do it again to finally hear of yer gratitude."

"Don't worry. You'll have to do it again and again and again. But something tells me you won't have any complaints."

"'Tis my husbandly duty." He winked at Kat. "I'll join ye. I've missed me family these past few days.

Shall we go see what they've been doing?"

Nick climbed out of bed and as Kat watched him, she thought she must be the luckiest girl in any century. He was the most beautiful man she'd ever seen, either naked or fully clothed. Before she could change her mind about what she was hungry for, she said, "I think that's a splendid idea."

As they arrived downstairs, the rest of the family were deep into their breakfast and hardly noticed them at first. Nick cleared his throat to get their attention.

"It's the two lovebirds," Duncan said. "We thought ye'd expired up there, 'tis been so long since we've seen ye."

"Come join us," Lettie said. "Tom, go get some food for Nick and Katriona, please."

"Yes, ma'am." Tom, one of the Mackall servants, hurried from the room.

Nick led Kat to her seat and he joined her at the table. There was an awkward silence as the two of them continued smiling and ogling each other.

"I can see that yer both feeling well, so I won't bother to ask after yer health," Aleck said, breaking the silence.

"Yes. We're wonderful," Kat answered. "How are you all? What's been going on?"

"We've been busy tending to our chores and Aleck is preparing to leave." Duncan nodded in Aleck's direction.

"What? Oh, no. I hardly got to spend any time with you," Kat complained.

"I ken ye were verra busy with yer new husband, as it should be. Unfortunately, I must return home today, but ye are welcome to come and visit me at any time and to stay as long as ye like. I look forward to getting to know me sister. We've much time to make up for." Aleck smiled warmly at Kat.

"Thank ye fer the invitation," Nick said. "We'll be sure to come stay with ye soon."

Aleck turned his attention to the matriarch of the Mackall Clan. "Yer all welcome, Lettie. We're family now. I want you to feel as at home in my castle as I've felt in yers. I'm grateful for the kind hospitality ye've extended to me and I'm looking forward to a lifetime of family gatherings both here and at Castle Sinclair."

Further down the table, Nick watched his sister Isla's reaction to Aleck's statement. He could tell she was doing her best to act like she didn't care one way or the other, but he knew her too well. She had taken a liking to his new brother-in-law. "I think me wee sister is quite taken with yer brother," Nick whispered to Kat.

"Do you really think so? She never looks particularly happy when he speaks to her." Kat's gaze wandered in Isla's direction.

"Aye. She is. Isla approaches love like it's a battle to be won. She thinks no one notices, but we are all on to her tactics. Yer brother is a man who can weather any attack she may plan. 'Twill be interesting to see what happens between them."

Kat checked her brother and could see his sideways glance as he sent it Isla's way. "I think Aleck may be smitten as well."

"We'll have to see what we can do to help the situation along," Nick said.

"Matchmaking, are you?" Kat teased. "And what's wrong with that?"

"Nothing. It just doesn't seem like a manly pursuit.

You may want to leave it up to me."

Instead of being insulted, Nick said, "Thank goodness. I was hoping you'd say that." He dug into the food which had just been placed in front of him.

"Thank you, Tom," Kat said as she received her trencher.

"Yer welcome, m'lady." Tom smiled shyly at Kat as he backed away.

"Mmm… I can't believe how hungry I am." Kat muttered between mouthfuls of food.

Conversation continued around them as they ate. Nick gazed up occasionally to see the others smiling at the two of them. He smiled back and then continued eating.

Once finished, he and Kat rose and, as if on cue, the rest of those at the table joined them.

"Nick, I wonder if I might spirit my sister away for a while so we can talk while I pack my things?" Aleck approached them and put an arm around Kat's shoulders.

"Of course. I have some things to see to, so take yer time. I'll see ye before ye leave." Nick leaned down and kissed Kat on the cheek and though he was loathe to leave her, he understood that she needed to spend some time with Aleck before he journeyed home.

"We'll see you in a while," Kat said as she lay her hand softly on his cheek.

"Aye. I'd best go before I'm not able." Nick motioned for his brothers to follow along and they quickly left the great hall for the courtyard.

"Well, I've things to see to as well. Isla, Merry, please join me." Lettie gathered her daughters and left Aleck and Kat behind. It didn't appear that Isla wished to leave, but her mother grasped her arm and pulled her along and out the doors.

"Shall we?" Aleck extended his arm for Kat to take. "Yes. I'm so sorry you'll be leaving today. I wish I could convince you to stay." Kat looked up at the handsome blonde-haired, green-eyed man who was in many ways a mirror image of herself.

"You probably could, but I really do have much to see to back home. I'll arrange with Nick for you to come visit soon. Then we'll have all the time we need to get to know each other better." He led her to the stairs and then up to his chambers. "For now, we can talk while I pack. I'm so happy this has not all been too much for you." Aleck opened the door and ushered Kat inside where she sat on the edge of his bed.

"It's been a lot to digest," Kat replied, "but it's mostly been good. I would have never met Nick and I would have never known I had a brother if I hadn't been brought back here by Ariweth. It was all worth it, even the horrible things I had to endure at the hands of Bearach Calhoun."

"Aye. It appears it was yer destiny." Nick folded some things and put them in his pack.

"I know what you mean. I've always believed that everything happens for a reason and if I hadn't been running away from Bearach Calhoun at that very moment, I may never have met Nick and, ultimately, I may not have met you." Kat felt sad about that for a moment, but then realized there was no need for sadness. Everything was perfect in her life right now and she felt it would continue to be. "And what of you, Aleck. What is your destiny?"

"I don't really know. I've always thought it was to be the laird of the Sinclair clan and I was happy with that. I don't know what else may be awaiting me."

"Have you ever thought about marrying?" Kat's matchmaking mission had begun.

"Aye. I've nae met the right woman yet. The other neighboring lairds have been parading their daughters in front of me for years, but there hasnae been a one that has caught me eye." He finished packing his clothing and set his bag on the floor, before sitting next to Kat. "Mayhap I've been too critical. I should probably just choose one and be done with it."

"No!" Kat exclaimed. "No! You shouldn't. You'll find the right lass. You'll see." She grabbed a piece of clothing and started folding. "What about Isla? What do you think of her?"

She could see from Aleck's expression that he was on to her. He knew exactly what she was up to. Apparently subtlety wasn't a strong suit for Kat. "Isla? I can see she's a beauty, but her temperament may need some work. I don't know if I'm up for the challenge."

"I think you'd be perfect together and something tells me you like a challenge. Besides, I know she seems persnickety, but I think if you put your mind to it, you could find the sweet, soft Isla that's just below the surface."

"Well, how will I ever know? I'm leaving verra soon and she rebuffed me the night of your wedding." Aleck stood and gave Kat his hand. He led her to the door and into the passageway.

"Don't you worry about it. Let me figure this out.

Nick and I will be visiting you soon and I think we could convince Lettie and the girls to join us. What do you think of that?" Kat waited hopefully for his answer.

"You know I'm looking forward to yer visit and I've already told the whole family they are welcome at any time." He carefully led Kat down the stairs and to the castle doors. "I give ye permission to meddle all ye like, sister." He chuckled as they went out into the courtyard, where he left his bag by the doors and then led Kat toward the stables. His men were congregated around the courtyard and when they saw Aleck, they all headed for their horses. "I see yer husband patiently waiting fer ye." Aleck pointed toward the stable doors, where

Nick leaned lazily against the building acting for all the world as if he hadn't noticed Kat walking towards him.

"Thank ye fer returning me wife to me," Nick said as he grabbed Kat around the waist, lifting her easily off the ground and spinning her around.

Kat steadied herself by placing her hands on his shoulders and while they were there, she enjoyed the feel of his strong muscles barely containing themselves beneath his surcoat. "Husband, I can see ye've missed me."

"More than ye ken," he lowered her so that her lips were in line with his and kissed her soundly before placing her back on the ground. "Aleck, 'tis been so short a time. Are ye on yer way then?"

"Aye. I'd best leave now. I'd like to travel a good distance home before dark." He took his sister's hand in his. "I'll be seeing ye soon I hope."

"Ye can be certain ye will," Nick assured him.

Aleck's horse was brought to him by one of the stableboys and he threw his pack up, securing it behind his saddle. Kissing Kat's cheek and then clapping Nick on the back, Aleck vaulted into his saddle and headed towards the gate with his men in tow. He gazed back as he left, waving his hand before disappearing from view.

Kat's eyes pricked with tears, which Nick quickly brushed away with his thumb. "Dinnae weep, love. We'll plan to see him again verra, verra soon."

"I know. It's just that I've never had a brother before and I'm not used to saying goodbye to him." Kat snuggled up under Nick's arm and he held her close, kissing the top of her head.

"'Tis the way of things here in this time. It will take work on our part to visit him so he'll know just how much you want to see him. Ye'll see. The time will go by as quickly as can be imagined." He pulled her close and they walked back to the castle.

Later that night, as they watched the Northern Lights from their bedchamber window, Nick reflected on the joy Kat had given him. He hadn't thought there was a woman alive who could win his heart, but somehow his sweet little wife had done just that. He'd loved her the moment he'd set eyes on her, of course he hadn't known it at the time, and that love was growing more and more each day.

"This is so beautiful," Kat said as they watched the colors moving through the night sky. "It looks like someone with an invisible paint brush is painting the most glorious scene just for our eyes."

"Mayhap they are." Nick stood behind her and wrapped his arms around Kat, holding her close to his heart.

Leaning down he kissed her at the sensitive spot on the side of her neck, the spot he'd discovered not so long ago. She sighed happily as his lips continued to explore her neck and then her shoulder. He'd enjoy finding all of Kat's secret places and he had a lifetime to do so.

"Come, wife. To bed."

Kat turned in his arms, gazing up at him and gifting him with a sweet, sensual smile. "Yes, husband. To bed."

THE END

Acknowledgments

Many thanks to my editor Vicki McGough for her help in editing this book.

I'd also like to thank my cover artist, Sheri McGathy, Covers by Sheri, for the beautiful work she did on the cover for Her Trusted Highlander.

Most of all I'd like to thank my family and friends for your support and encouragement throughout this process.

About the Author

Jennae was born and raised a New England girl, just outside of Boston, Massachusetts, where her imagination was always bigger than she was. Surrounded by an abundance of nostalgic, historical landmarks, her love of history and creative writing was formed. Her large extended Irish and Italian families were not only a great source of support and inspiration, but her home was always filled with laughter, love, lots of good food and amazing story telling.

After years of wearing many different career caps, Jennae was determined to do something she had always loved and her vivid imagination took over once again as she decided to follow her dream of writing stories that tapped into her love of magical people and places.

Jennae now lives in the San Francisco Bay Area with her husband, where they've raised two beautiful and talented children. Along the way they've gathered a menagerie of pets, including dogs, cats, chickens and horses to make their family complete.

To connect with Jennae:

@jealil JennaeValeAuthor

www.jennaevaleauthor.com jennaevaleauthor@gmail.com

Also by Jennae Vale

The Thistle & Hive Series Book 1 - A Bridge Through Time

Book 2 - A Thistle Beyond Time Book 3 - Separated By Time Book 4 - A Matter of Time

www.ingramcontent.com/pod-product-compliance
Lightning Source LLC
Chambersburg PA
CBHW071133200626
46817CB00018B/2932

* 9 780099 700643 8 *